Praise fc
The Grace Church Mystery Series

DEATH IN THE OLD RECTORY

"I enjoyed *Death in the Old Rectory* so much that at times I found myself laughing out loud because each character brought personality to the story. I visualized the scenes as if watching a live performance where each character played their part extremely well. As Detective Joyce and Officer Chen, along with Lester (an unofficial security and criminal expert), begin to uncover the clues of the murder, the fun and adventure begin."

—Vernita Naylor for Readers' Favorite Reviews

DEATH IN THE MEMORIAL GARDEN

"Lovable characters, atmospheric charm, and sins from the past make this a must for brick & murder readers."

—Mary Daheim, author of the Bed-and-Breakfast Mysteries and the Alpine/Emma Lord Mysteries

"A heart-warming story filled with likeable characters as they deal with murder, mishaps, and mayhem. An insightful view into the challenges faced by today's urban churches. I look forward to the next murder at Grace Church."

—Liz Osborne, author of *Dirty Laundry,* A Robyn Kelly Mystery

"Deviny had a challenge on her hands and she met it and exceeded it. With her character development, her take on a subject that is divisive with the Church, and solid pacing I'm looking forward to more installments with the other characters taking their turn in the spotlight. Recommended."

—Vikki Walton, I Love a Mystery

5 Stars: "This book is so good it practically reads itself. Let me tell you a secret. I was very tired as I read this, but this book was so exciting that I could not sleep! I did not nod off once. If you like mysteries, this book is for you. It is practically squeaky clean, and it is enjoyable reading for a winter's night."

—My Devotional Thoughts

"A fast-paced tale that has intrigue, mystery and humor all rolled up into a neat little story that takes place over a span of one week .... the story-line has surprising twist and turns coupled with satirical humor that will keep you engaged, and a quirky cast of characters who are a lot of fun."

—Jersey Girl Book Reviews

"I just loved following the day-to-day activities of this crazy group that is keeping Grace Church running on a wing and a prayer! Author Kathie Deviny does a great job creating three-dimensional characters, not only the aspects of them that play into the solving of the mystery but random miscellaneous traits that simply make them REAL."

—Words by Webb

"I did enjoy the casual nature of this story and it was short enough that I read it in one sitting. If you are looking for something to read while relaxing – this is the book. I give this book a 4 out of 5 stars."

—The Stuff of Success

"If you are a member of a small, older church, you will definitely relate to the characters of the altar guild, vestry and organist.... The book is humorous, satirical in the right places and a lively little read. I highly recommend it for a light afternoon read!"

—Bless Their Hearts Mom

"A great cozy.... with a big mystery to solve and colorful characters. I look forward to reading her next book!"

—Book Lovers Stop

5 Stars: "I love a nice, cozy mystery! This novel had some wonderfully eccentric characters; Daniel the organist was my personal favorite. Set in an Episcopalian church, the mystery is reminiscent of Agatha Christie's

'Miss Marple' series, except this time, instead of villagers, we have church members. Very nicely done; I hope this is the first in a series."

—The Self-Taught Cook

"There were many revelations, twists and turns that I was not expecting. Deviny weaves a charming mystery that can be read in one sitting."

—Wanted Readers Blogspot

"A very light-hearted mystery, not too much depth involved with the characters or the location. I would definitely recommend this to all readers of cozy mysteries."

—A Date with a Book

"A fun and quick read. It makes me smile to reflect on it!"

—Beth Art from the Heart

"A fun, cozy mystery that combines two threads: a whodunit and a drive to save a valuable community resource …. A very quick read with characters who will capture your heart. It's the perfect way to spend an afternoon relaxing."'

—Popcorn Reads

Death on
Sacred Ground

Death on
Sacred Ground

A Grace Church Mystery

~~~

KATHIE DEVINY

**CAMEL
PRESS**

Kenmore, WA

CAMEL
PRESS

A Camel Press book published by Epicenter Press

Epicenter Press
6524 NE 181st St.
Suite 2
Kenmore, WA 98028

For more information go to:
www.Camelpress.com
www.Coffeetownpress.com
www.Epicenterpress.com
www.KathieDeviny.com

Design by Scott Book and Melissa Vail Coffman

Death on Sacred Ground

ISBN: 978-1-60381-717-2 (Trade Paper)
ISBN: 978-1-60381-718-9 (eBook)

Printed in the United States of America

In Loving Memory
Terry W. Deviny

Acknowledgments

JAN ROBITSCHER, MASTER OF DIVINITY, SERVES on the faculty of School for Deacons in Berkeley, CA, and is also a spiritual director. She advised me on the issues facing persons with low sight. She let me know that properly trained guide dogs would never bark at someone who stepped on their toes, as happens in the first chapter. Possibly they would yelp. She also advocated for Rev. Catherine and Louette to play a larger role in identifying the murderers. Now they do.

The "dedicated staff" of Santa Barbara, California's community blog, Edhat.com inspired my portrayal of the Central Seattle website. Special thanks to Rodger Dodger, their scanner jockey and philosopher, who inspired my character Bill Bailey. The Capitol Hill Blog in Seattle was another good resource.

The Carpinteria Ca writers' group, which I attend much of the year, has supported my efforts with the right amount of applause and constructive criticism. Special thanks to Suzanne Ahn, Mike Winneguth, Ted Baum, Phoenix Hocking, Mike Frey, Julia Offen, Rodney Chen, and Sue Perry, great authors all.

Jennifer McCord, for her no-nonsense mentoring and support.

And to Paul, always.

Chapter One

~~~

"**W**HERE'S MY STUFF?" ASKED FATHER ROBERT Vickers, looking around his office the morning he returned to work.

The rector of Grace Church in Seattle had returned from a three-week honeymoon, which hadn't nearly been long enough. He felt a strong urge to jump out the South facing window even though it was covered with white-flowered vines this mid-September day. Henry, his sentimental sexton, thought what he called morning glory was pretty, but Robert knew better. It was the insidious Northwest bindweed, which grew about a foot an hour and would soon force its way through the casings and twine around his bookshelves.

The desk was there and his chair, and the other furniture, but where were the piles of papers that comprised his filing system, the ones that had been scattered over the floor when he had left? And where were the various items that had covered his desk, most importantly the picture of his new wife, Molly?

"Before you begin your day, Father, would you like a cup of tea?"

"I desperately need a cup, Adele. Especially if it's that smoky Lapsong Soochong. I'm sure that the Saints are drinking it in heaven, even if it comes from the East. But where's my stuff?"

Adele Evans, his volunteer parish administrator reminded him, "Father, you insisted that Reverend Catherine use your office while you were away. You said that you wanted her to have all the authority of the rector. Well, we had to clear the floor, so she wouldn't trip. You'll notice that your files are ringing the room. We chose Daniel to move them because of his Per, fectionism." The reason for her speech hesitation was the stroke she'd suffered after Nick's murder last year.

"He spent over an hour categorizing. He'll be here sh,shortly to move them back for you. And Reverend Catherine and Louette will be here at ten to debrief."

Robert gave her his best crinkly-eyed smile. "Bless you, Adele. You're providing the same volunteer service for me that my Molly is for the Bishop. After Catherine and I have discussed the pastoral concerns, could you join us while we debrief the administrative hassles, of which I know there have been many."

His smile disappeared. "I never expected my honeymoon to be punctuated by Skype calls about things that could have waited a few weeks. And believe me, I don't blame Catherine. The word's gotten out that Grace Church is planning to develop the corner of our property, so the planners and developers are lining up and the community activists are right behind them, and I'm going to need a translator to understand the terms they use: Upzoning, downzoning, market rate, parking allocation, offsets, air rights—"

Sensing the beginning of a mini-rant that would threaten her carefully prepared welcome back schedule, Adele interjected, "Father Robert, I n-notice you're not wearing a clerical shirt today." She'd noticed that he was wearing a neatly pressed blue checkered number.

Last year, her tone would have been critical. This year, she was just interested. He wasn't sure if he should tell her the reason, which was that he couldn't bring himself to put on his clerical persona just yet. He was suffering a severe case of post-honeymoon letdown.

He decided on the half-truth. "I guess going from a t-shirt to clergy shirt was too much for my first day back. Molly noticed that there were no civilian shirts in my wardrobe, so she took us on a shopping trip to Nordstrom. I have two more just like this one."

Waiting for Adele to bring back the tea, he thought about the past two years. Grace Church's tottering bell tower was now repaired, and the Memorial Garden had reverted from a death site back to a resting place for the deceased of the parish. And the Old Rectory now honored Nick's memory as the drop-in center and office for their food bank.

But they were still in a financial hole, and were struggling to maintain the historic structure, built in the late nineteenth century to house one of the city's first Protestant congregations.

Robert knew they would have to develop the corner of the property containing the Old Rectory and the former gymnasium now being used as a food bank. He just didn't know if he had the fire to shepherd his flock through this next phase, which was certain to bring forth long buried sentiments of all kinds. He was certain there were a few parishioners that would throw themselves in front of any bulldozer trying to eliminate the sacred Old Rectory and gymnasium, even though they were standing on their last legs and brought no needed income to the parish.

Why not discuss this next step with Adele while they had tea? She could suggest names for a support group, like the ones that had formed around him after the tragic deaths at the church. This time he needed members with business expertise who could also corral his tendency to drift away when it was time to move from creative planning to productive work.

Having a sympathetic group had certainly worked to see them through those two tragedies. You couldn't say they'd solved the deaths, but the force of a diverse group had created a synergy that allowed those things to happen. Was that a bit of energy he was feeling?

BEFORE HE'D HAD TIME to enjoy more than an inch of tea, three men burst into the outer office, nearly knocking over a woman and her leashed black lab.

"They're here!" yelled Henry, the longtime church sexton, tripping over one of the dog's paws and receiving a yelp. Lester, the night sexton, and Terry, the food bank manager, pulled him upright.

"What the heck's going on?" yelled Father Robert, his lap full of Lapsong Soochong. Henry continued to splutter, and Terry and Lester apologized to the dog and woman.

As Adele jumped up to get a cloth, Lester stepped forward. "Father," and turning back, "Rev. Catherine, allow me to take charge here while Henry and Terry get themselves composed. The *they* that Henry refers to are two firemen and one firewoman from Station Number Two."

"It's Station Three, not Two," Henry corrected.

"In whatever case," continued Lester, "these three have arrived to do a thorough safety inspection, top to bottom, of the Old Rectory and the food bank."

Robert put his head in his hands. "And you just left them standing around while you—"

The Reverend Catherine Brown stepped forward. She was dressed in blue jeans, a black shirt and clerical collar, and was wearing thick lens glasses; she had a genetic eye disease, and her guide dog, Louette, protected her from trips, falls, and more serious collisions.

"Louette and I passed by their rig parked in front of the Old Rectory. I could just make out these guys blocking the entrance to the door. I gave a few hand signals to let the firefighters know we'd be there in a minute."

Robert's head rose. He was nearsighted himself and admired her poise in handling situations like this. "Good job, Catherine. Now, what are you all so riled up about?"

Now Terry was the spokesman. The forty-year-old food bank director was a slender man and favored eye-catching clothing. Case in point, his neon green baseball cap. "Father, you can't have forgotten the warning we got last time they showed up. The boxes piled ten high in the basement and at the food bank, the extension cords running everywhere, the paints and chemicals stored where they shouldn't be.

"And now we've turned the Old Rectory into an unofficial drop in and hygiene center for the neighborhood, complete with the commercial-sized hot water heater, washer and dryer that Stacy got donated."

Robert nodded. Stacy Chase, descended from one of Seattle's founding families, with degrees in marketing and business administration, was the church's fundraiser par-excellence.

Terry continued, "So now the fuses blow once a day or so at the rectory and the food bank. And no offense, Lester, but someone needs to teach you how to pick up after yourself." The formerly homeless Lester lived on the rectory's top floor and hadn't yet mastered kitchen and laundry etiquette.

Robert was pacing around the office floor, since his chair was soggy with tea.

"I remember when they came last time, but that was during the investigation of Nick's murder and they gave us a reprieve because the area was a crime scene. He looked over at the white-flowered window and felt a second urge to jump out. "I guess the reprieve is over."

"Father," Catherine said, deliberately using his title. "It's not as if nothing's been done. You left their report for me with the other pending projects. Adele and I have created a correction plan, and since Arlis is onsite at the rectory, she's been helping. I think you'll find no more extension cords or space heaters. We haven't had time to tackle the basement. They should give us another extension since we're making progress."

She trained her gaze, hugely magnified by her glasses' lenses, on Henry and Lester. "And I was waiting for the corrective action reports I asked you for two weeks ago, before giving Father my update." For a good ten seconds the two were frozen like deer in the headlights.

She grinned. "Stand down, guys. How was I to know they'd come today? Don't you think we'd all better go over and face the music?"

Robert laughed. "With you at my side, Catherine, I can't wait. And remember, it's Robert."

Chapter Two

～～

ARLIS BELL, THE CHURCH'S BOOKKEEPER AND computer whiz, had already unplugged and hidden the space heater she wasn't supposed to be using. She was single, her early thirties, and dressed in drab, slouchy clothes. Her straight hair was an uninteresting brown, but it framed thick eyebrows and hazel eyes that turned down a bit at the corner, emphasizing her waif-like looks. Arlis's style was influenced by her love of all things French, developed during the two years she had studied in Paris.

Because their names both started with A and had two syllables, Arlis was often confused with. Father Robert's assistant and long-time parishioner Adele, who dressed smartly in colorful outfits, permed her hair and was the same age as Arlis' mother.

She was prepared for the fire inspection in the next fifteen minutes or so, which she would facilitate to the best of her ability. The windows in her corner office, formerly one of the Old Rectory's bedrooms, had a fine view of the intersection below, so she'd both heard and seen the fire truck roll to a stop in front. She had no guilt whatsoever about disobeying Rev. Catherine's instructions. The drafty old structure issued the bare minimum of heat from its radiators, and the air was not only chilly but damp.

She'd suffered from bronchitis and allergies all her life, probably because she'd grown up in another ill-heated, damp old pile North on Capitol Hill. She was all in for implementing the other fire department regulations and ruthlessly policed extension cords and potentially flammable materials. But if she was going to work here, the heater was staying.

It had been hilarious to see Lester, Terry and Henry trying to hold off the fire inspectors with their scrawny bodies. She'd run down to the stair landing for a look and saw Rev. Catherine give the unwelcome visitors the high sign.

Her French-infused mind declared *bonne chance* that Rev. Catherine had been selected to fill in for Father Robert during his honeymoon. Father Robert, *Dieu l'aime*, was more dreamer than organizer. How was he going to explain to the inspectors the piles of Mad magazines in the dry fir attic, his former lodgings? He hadn't had time to move them to his new home yet.

And all the decrepit furniture offloaded by parishioners for use in the rectory, now piled in the basement? Father Robert hadn't wanted to offend anyone by donating the stash to Goodwill. And all the empty boxes collected by Adele when she ran the thrift shop, just in case? She'd heard Rev. Catherine tell Lester to break them down and put them in the recycle bin, but of course he had more creative uses for his time, like visiting his old cronies who stood at the freeway entrance with begging signs.

Her one worry was that her volunteer job had asked her to fill a shift today. She was a moderator for an online message board, which required constant vigilance to comments posted to the site. No one, not even her two bosses, Father Robert and Terry, knew about her other life. It wasn't that she was neglecting the technical support and book-keeping duties she performed for both the church and food bank. She arrived to work on time and was at her desk for a full shift. And since she'd become a member of Grace church six months ago, after Nick's murder, she made herself available following Sunday services to cut the necessary check or whatever.

It was up to her, with minimal guidance from the self-described "dedicated staff" of the Central Seattle Message Board to delete any comment that violated what were constantly evolving boundaries of language, taste, and legibility.

The Central Seattle Message Board was an Internet forum. "Posters" could hold conversations by means of messages responding to earlier messages. Unlike Facebook, the conversations related to an event or topic, not a person. The first poster to ask a question or make a comment started what was called a thread, usually listed in order of time posted.

Some form of registration was required to comment, but posters didn't have to reveal their identity. People who didn't register could lurk, meaning read whatever was posted. The Central Seattle Message Board covered more area than most, both above and below the I-5 freeway as it wound through downtown Seattle. Its territory included the county courthouse and jail, public housing projects, three hospitals, and highrise luxury condominiums.because comments could be posted anonymously, the site was hounded by trolls, commenters who liked to sow discord, and when she was on what she called Nanny Duty, Arlis made at least one deletion per day. On her own, she would have deleted many more posts, but when she'd first moderated on a trial basis, the dedicated staff told her she was too prudish. Only comments that were indecently gross, libelous, or totally non-factual were eligible for deletion.

You just never knew when an innocuous item about a city councilman visiting a preschool would prompt some scumbag (a term beloved by many Central Seattle posters) to suggest how cool it would be if they could spend their days holding preschoolers on their laps. And that had happened, just last week, and she'd almost missed it. It would have cost her her unpaid job, the main source of satisfaction in her secluded life.

She also had to ride herd on Bill Bailey, the site's also-unpaid "scanner guy," who reported everything of interest gleaned from the multiple police and emergency frequencies he monitored. Even though she'd never met him and didn't know where he lived, they'd become friends of sorts via text messaging.

They couldn't be more different. Bill was a self-described 230 pound, 6' tall vet with a bad back, whose employment had been irregular at best after his discharge from the Air Force. She suspected he survived on disability payments.

Bill had a heart of gold and was a natural writer. Besides his scanner posts, he issued forth stream of consciousness essays on everything from his life in the foster care system to what was happening on the streets of Seattle. He rarely, if ever, swore or flamed out on his posts. He was all business, issuing multiple updates on, say, the progress of a police chase on I-5, through the University District, and ending with an arrest at Northgate.

The problem was that he took great offense when someone posted a criticism of his reporting. Like today, he'd committed the sin of misspelling congregate as *congrigate*. It was probably just a typo, because his spelling was head and shoulders above most of the commenters.

Bill had blasted the person who'd corrected him with both barrels, asking how long #234 could hold his pee while reporting on five incidents at once. Then the game was on. The whole subject changed from the homeless *congregating* at a certain corner to whether Bill deserved to be dissed like that. That took up 25 posts. She didn't interfere with his complaints, because he seemed to get great satisfaction when his fans shut down the complainers.

In any event, Arlis never knew when her nanny services would be needed. Right now, things were quiet. She turned things over to one of the dedicated staff and went back down the Old Rectory stairs to facilitate the inspection.

Everyone was gathered in the former living room of the Old Rectory and had just finished introducing themselves when she heard the ping of a text coming in. She peeked at her screen and gasped. A fire had broken out in what was called the Homeless Jungle, a few blocks to the South and just above the freeway.

"What is it?" Robert asked. She hesitated and then told him, since the jungle was so near, and they all knew how quickly fire could spread. While she was talking, all the fire inspectors' radios went off. As they ran out the door one of them called back, "How did you get the word before we did?"

Without answering, Arlis ran up the first flight of the Old Rectory's stairs and disappeared around the landing.

Father Robert asked Terry, "What's going on?"

"I have no idea," said Terry. "For the last few months, she's hardly left her laptop. Maybe she's started monitoring the police and fire scanners. Lester, what do you know?"

Lester had pulled the blinds back from a West-facing window and was looking down the steep hill towards the freeway. He turned around.

"One year ago, it could've been me over in that burning jungle, deciding whether to run for it or help my fellow campers. You don't think I could take a break from my duties here to see if I can—"

"No, Lester," answered both Robert and Rev. Catherine. She waved her hand signaling Robert to continue, saying "Oops" under her breath. Robert grinned. "No problem, sister," and continued, "Lester, please run over to the corner to see if smoke is coming our way. If we get an evacuation order, I need you here to make sure everyone leaves. Then get out the hoses and watch the perimeter. See if you can coordinate with the halfway house." Many years ago, Grace Church had offered the property they owned in the next block to an organization providing housing for parolees. "If the fire department orders you to evacuate, come down to the condo. I think the rest of us should err on the safe side and gather there. That's where we'll be."

He paused. "Oops, is that OK Catherine? The condo is your home now."

"Of course," she said, "and I think it will make a perfect command post ."

Not really her home, she reflected, just a nice place to stay while she'd filled in for Father . Robert. She'd be moving back to Olympia, sixty miles south, within the week.

Grace Church's deacon Mary Martin stuck her head in the front door. "I just got a text from Arlis about the fire. If you don't need me here, I'll go across the street to the retirement tower. I'm sure quite a few of the residents are looking out their windows at the smoke and beginning to freak out. Thank God it's Daniel's day off and we don't need to drag him away from the organ."

Terry said, "I'll make sure nobody's left in the food bank and then make sure Arlis is out of her office. We'll meet you at Rev. Catherine's." Seeing Arlis come down the stairs lugging her laptop and a strongbox, he said, "I amend my statement. Good job, Arlis. Head out with the rest to Rev. Catherine's and I'll join you after I sweep the foodbank."

"CATHERINE, YOU'VE GOT THIS place looking fantastic," Robert exclaimed as they entered the condo located four blocks North of the church. He'd lived there before marrying Molly, after the Old Rectory became a thrift shop and offices. The condo had been donated to the church by the daughter of recently deceased parishioners. She'd moved to the Seattle suburbs to be near her unfortunate husband, who was lodged at the local penitentiary

Catherine had rearranged the furniture to create a cozy sitting area, including a soft bed for her service dog Louette. Scatter rugs, lamp cords and anything else that presented a tripping hazard had been removed, which gave the space a light, airy feel. She announced, "Boy, are you all lucky. I just happened to stop by the Hilltop Bakery yesterday and managed not to eat all the cookies. Would one of you mind putting them on a plate and turning on the coffee pot? There's tea, also."

"We've got our own little church command post set up," said Robert. "I guess the first thing to do is call the Bishop to alert him." He did so and was able to kill the proverbial two birds because his new wife Molly was the Bishop's secretary.

"He's off visiting St. Aiden's in Bellingham" Molly told him, "but I'll let him know. Are you OK?"

"For a first day back at work, it's been pretty eventful. But Catherine's got the daily operations under control and our Arlis seems to have inside information about the fire, so—"

He was interrupted by Arlis' gasp.

"They've found a body!"

Chapter Three

~~~

SEATTLE'S HOMELESS JUNGLE IS CERTAINLY NOT unique. The word jungle has been used since the nineteenth century to describe the places where the homeless, mostly men, but also women in recent times, form outdoor encampments. The residents have been referred to as hobos, tramps, bums and, more recently, campers.

In the industrial town of Everett, thirty miles to the North of Grace Church, the jungle is treeless, located among the warehouses lining the Snohomish River. In England, the term Gypsy appeared in the fourteenth century, derived from *Egyptian*. Then came Vagabond, and more recently Traveler, or New Age Traveler. There don't seem to be jungles in England, just vacant land and urban "squats."

However, Seattle's jungle is unique in that much of it is in the remnants of the city's deciduous forest. Seattle is a city of steep hills, and patches above the I-5 freeway are too steep for building. Since the city's annual rainfall is only slightly lower than the nearby rainforest on the Olympic Peninsula, the firs, pines, alders, madrone, and maple grow lushly and provide good cover.

Violent death happens in every conceivable location, from mansions to alleyways, from bars to the high seas. No one should be surprised that it also happens in homeless encampments.

THE VICTIM'S BODY HAD probably been moved to the site of the fire, evidenced by its battered condition. Because of the wet tinder, the fire sent out lots of smoke and was spotted quickly. The medical examiner hadn't released the cause of death.

The Grace Church command post learned all of this within an hour of the first fire call, thanks to Arlis' mysterious updates.

With the arrival of aid cars, fire trucks and police, the jungle's residents had fled in all directions, some up the hill towards the hospital and public housing project, some down underneath the freeway bridge, others jumping over guardrails onto the freeway itself. Traffic stood still in both directions of I-5.

AFTER THE IMMEDIATE DANGER was past, Lester disobeyed. Father Robert's instructions walked away from Henry's screeching and Terry's entreaties, and went into the jungle with his German Shepherd, Spike. Spike had been his constant companion on the streets well before he was offered the night sexton job at the church. Spike served double duty as a deterrent to various threats and as service dog. He'd had no formal training but had learned to help his poor-sighted master keep his balance and self-respect.

There was police tape everywhere, blocking Lester's usual entry points to the jungle. He and Spike walked North and found Seattle Police detective Raymond Chen stationed outside the public housing tower. Raymond provided off duty security at Grace Church's food bank and had also worked on the previous deaths at the church. He had Lester's trust and respect, insofar as that was possible.

Detective Chen greeted Lester with a hand slap. "Hey, bro, are you still wearing that ragged flannel shirt? With your new respectable job?"

Lester ignored this and asked, "Who was—"

Raymond talked over him. "Man, you're employed now. Get a new shirt or ask them for a uniform. And get a haircut. You look like—"

"Who was it?" Lester interrupted. "Let me in there and I might be able to help you."

"Everyone's left," Raymond said, "including the deceased."

Lester asked, "He wasn't Native American, was he?"

"'You mean the deceased? Wait, do you mean the guy you used to hang out with?"

"Yea, Pete. The last time I saw him was more than a year ago, when we were at the Old Rectory with everyone who helped find out who killed bird lady Clare. Father Robert was so thankful that he said he'd give both of us jobs at the church. When the get-together was over, we both walked down the hill, not yet having any firm place to lay our heads for the night."

Raymond let him reminisce for thirty seconds. "So then?"

"So, then he was going to head to the Salish Center for the night. I wouldn't be acceptable there, so I told him I was taking Spike to the dog run above the freeway.

And I didn't see him after that night. I got my job and lodging at the Old Rectory and I later found out his tribe up North ordered him back for their version of rehab." He looked heavenward, as he always did when referring to the Almighty "God has helped me not to succumb to alcohol, and He's also—" Seeing Raymond's narrowed eyes, Lester changed tack.

"Anyway, I heard that tribe, whose name I can't remember, sent him back here a few weeks ago to help his brothers—and maybe some sisters—teaching them how to make money by carving those pretty wood animals and other things. I went looking for him at the Salish Center, but they aren't talking. 'Probably figured I'd lure him back to the bad way."

Raymond tensed up and his voice grew louder. "I hope he's keeping his knife in its sheath or whatever he keeps it in. You know about the guy that was shot by one of my fellow officers for brandishing a knife, and before you start arguing about holding versus brandishing, let me tell you—"

Lester intervened, "Let's work on this together, bro, which deflated Raymond.

"Lester, for God knows whatever reason I trust you on this. So, I'll tell you a few things, but if I hear you've snitched me off, you'd better plan to move out of town too. Number one, the deceased was a white male, age forty or so. No id or phone on him and we're waiting for the print results. His appearance and clothing didn't look like someone who slept outside. And number two, cause of death appears to be a knife wound—not the usual pen knife or switchblade, but one with a longer, curved blade, you know, like—"

To Raymond's astonishment, Lester nodded, and said, "Pete would never use his carving knife to kill someone and neither would his fellow carvers, of which there are many in Seattle. That would be like a disere— I mean, a desecration. Rev. Catherine told me how to pronounce that word the right way, because I use it so much. She—"

Raymond cut Lester off. "She's something else, agreed. So, who else would use a knife with a curved blade?"

"Maybe someone wants to throw us off the track to make it seem that one of our original peoples were responsible." Lester rubbed his eyes, which Raymond thought were badly in need of glasses.

His thoughts changed course dramatically. Here was a reason to contact Arlis, whom he hoped to get to know better. She probably administered the church's health care insurance. He doubted that Lester knew he was entitled to glasses.

He attempted a course correction. "You know, Les, that term original people sounds a lot better than indigenous or native. I'll have to remember that."

Lester spit on the ground, letting Raymond know that he'd gone too far down the good buddy path.

"Now, as your official consulting citizen, I'll tell you two things. With all your computer skills you can look up the rest. The first thing is that knife blades curve both up and down, and the blades are all different lengths and widths, depending on what they're used for. And as for what they're used for, as I just said, you can look those up. But just for one, you'll find them onboard most every fishing boat. The second thing is that I have a feeling the outsider that was killed was acting as a sort of scout."

Raymond asked, "Is this one of your intuitions or based on some facts? Have any new groups been hanging around lately?"

"Think about it, man," Lester answered. "Think about all those Green Streeters and preservationists and gentrificators that have been plastering signs all over saying 'No Development' and 'Smart Development' and planting flowers around the street signs and protesting for and against tearing down old buildings. And the latest group? They've been hanging around for about a month. I call them the Urban Foresters. Your dead body was probably one of them."

"I know most of those terms, but what's a Green Streeter?" asked Raymond. He'd pulled out his phone and started a search.

"Now you've got me interested. Here they are, with a bunch of different names. Some of them are only interested in preserving big old street trees, which they say provide 'façade greening,' and some are turning parking strips into gardens. My goodness, the others are trying to link up every tree and bush for a thousand miles into a trail that goes from Alaska to California. Not up in the mountains but right through the cities and towns. They call it a 'Greenway.' Here's a map that shows all the public bathrooms and hostels and other free stuff along the way. You're the man, Lester. Let me know what else you learn. And I'm not making you a snitch. You're a fully employed tax paying citizen, so I won't have to pay you, like we do the others. On the other hand, we do pay our consultants, which you are on the road to being."

Lester started to spit again, then stopped and turned toward the Old Rectory. "Come on, Spike. Time for dinner."

Chapter Four

~~~

FATHER ROBERT, UNAWARE THAT LESTER HAD deserted his post, deactivated the church's mini command post at 5:30 and was home with Molly by 6. He had a hard time believing he was living in this Northwest modern split-level overlooking a greenbelt and just a few miles from Grace Church. When Molly's first husband died, she'd decided to stay in the compact but well-designed structure and had been thrilled that Robert agreed to join her there after they were married.

Robert had changed into a t-shirt with the church's *Grace Abounds* logo and sweatpants. His new wife stayed in her work clothes, a red cashmere sweater and well-fitting designer jeans, to his pleasure.

He briefed her on the fire and the discovery of the body.

"Oh, no! God bless his soul." She put her forkful of chicken back down. "I'm afraid everyone will blame one of the homeless campers. As if they weren't already being assaulted and robbed themselves.

"And just think, dear," she continued, "a week ago we were basking in the sun in Santa Barbara, and smugly commenting that the homeless there didn't have a big forest to camp in, only the narrow bushy area next to the freeway, and thinking how sweet it was that so many were living in all those old motor homes parked by the beach. Remember the one who put a potted plant outside on the sidewalk? And the voice floating out wishing me 'Happy Mother's Day' even though it was September."

They fell into reminiscence about their wedding, reception, and honeymoon. After the ceremony, conducted by the Bishop at full volume,

everyone had adjourned to the Parish Hall. The crowd spilled out into
the Memorial Garden, where a brass band was playing.

"Remember Terry's guessing game?" Robert asked. The church's food
bank director, wearing a garish Hawaiian shirt, had taken the mic, and
asked,

"Where are Neola and Fred? "

"Underneath the tuba," yelled Henry, who would never forget his
shovel's encounter with a wooden crate while digging a hole for Neola's
ashes. The subsequent uproar from the family and other mourners had
begun the saga they called "Death in the Memorial Garden."

Terry shouted, "and where is Mae?"

"Over there by the Rhody," Arlis had answered, "next to —." She'd
choked, then managed to finish, "next to Nick." Mae and Nick had both
volunteered at the thrift shop located on the first floor of the Old Rectory
and, despite their age difference, had become fast friends.

After Nick's brutal murder and internment in the Memorial Garden,
Mae had insisted on being interred next to him when her time came.
Nick's burly physique, kindness and charm had earned him other admir-
ers, including the much younger Arlis.

When the reception finally wound down, the newlyweds had gone
home for a good night's sleep. After a leisurely breakfast, they'd headed
South on the 1-5 freeway in Molly's red Fiat. Robert's 1985 VW diesel
Rabbit, the only takeaway from his first marriage, was not up to the
challenge.

Molly, a longtime Seattleite, pointed out her favorite landmarks: the
preserved smokestacks from the original city steam plant, now home to
a biotech company; the old Rainier brewery, now a storage facility; and
the old public health hospital, repurposed first for Amazon and now for
medical and educational programs.

When they reached Portland, Oregon, Robert took over, since he'd
served a parish there before relocating to Seattle. The main attraction
for him was Powell's Bookstore, with its miles of books, but they also
visited Forest Park, overlooking the city with its world-famous Rose and
Japanese Gardens.

The next day, they'd walked the sand at Cannon Beach, Oregon, over-
whelmed by Haystack Rock and its tidepools. Their next stopover was
Eureka, California, where they were enchanted by the turbulent ocean
and the Redwood forest. Their final travel day included visits to the

Spanish Mission in San Louis Obispo and a local winery, then on to their beachside hotel in Santa Barbara.

THEY WERE NOW IN the living room and had turned on the fire.

Robert said, "I wish Seattle had a great breakfast place like the one that showed the surfing videos."

"Yes, and the long pier and lovely weather," added Molly. "Wouldn't it be great to spend some time there every year? Maybe we could do a house exchange."

Robert, whose psychological glass was at half empty, said, "Who'd want to visit Seattle in the winter?"

"If they were skiers they might."

Robert stood up. "Let me get out some ice cream for dessert, and we'll continue this conversation. If we wait any longer it'll be too easy for us, or at least, me to settle back into the same old routine."

Dipping into a bowl of full fat vanilla bean, he asked, "How about this? Maybe Catherine and I could be co-rectors. Catherine is wonderful. It drives me crazy that she hasn't found a full-time job."

Molly answered, "I think we could arrange a donation from the Ferguson Trust till next July. Then the congregation will have to decide."

"Would you?" asked her husband.

"Yes," answered his wife, "but remember, I'm bringing you into the foundation, so you'll also have a say. One of our goals is to promote health in medically underserved communities. Catherine could, and should, incorporate that into the development project." Then she changed tack. "I like your idea of tapering off work. But why wait for two years? There's no reason for you to work for pay any longer."

"And you'd desert Bishop Anthony?"

"Robert! How many times have I told you, he's retiring next spring?"

"But I'm too young to retire!"

"Robert, Robert." Molly was frustrated now. "Step away and think about how you want to spend the rest of your life, which is well over half over. I don't mean living the life of Riley, being part of the one or five or ten percent. I mean living a life suited to your gifts whether or not there's a paycheck attached."

He wasn't ready to give her an answer. To his shame, he said, "OK dear, I'll think about that."

AFTER EVERYONE LEFT HER temporary lodging, Catherine replaced her teacup with a full wine glass. She needed Merlot to wind down her days, not so much from her duties, but the loneliness that had been her companion for as long as she could remember. Even her dear dog Louette couldn't take that away.

Today's doings, which she had relished, made her want to share them with a friend or companion. She couldn't think of anyone, and in the absence of anyone, remembered the man in the wheelchair she'd met at divinity school ten years ago. Even with her low vision she could see his eyes sparkle and knew that he was trying his best to engage her. She remembered her attraction and then her repulsion. *He was disabled. As if she weren't. He said they'd be a good team. He'd be the eyes and she'd have his back. She hadn't let it happen.*

Her sojourn at Grace church had allowed her to exercise every aspect of her ministry as an Episcopal Priest. During the week, the adaptive programs on her computer allowed her to keep well on top of the administrative duties. On Sundays, Lester edged her into the correct place following the choir and checked that the bow Louette wore on top of her collar was straight. Sweet Daniel coordinated the rhythm of the entrance hymn to her steps.

Now that Robert, the church's full-time rector, was back from his honeymoon, she'd have to find another temporary situation, filling in for another priest on vacation or sick leave. Gulping her wine, she vowed she wouldn't settle for another low paying gig, filling in for three weeks at the tiny mission near the fishing town of Westport, and then two weeks in Mount Vernon to the North, and so on, which she had to supplement with her disability payment.

She didn't want just a job either, not after ten years employment at a non-profit dedicated to disability rights, her Master of Divinity degree from General Seminary in New York City and her subsequent ordination as a priest. She'd interviewed for many entry level church positions but realized they were afraid they couldn't cope with her disability. She wouldn't accept that anymore. She wanted a full-time career in the church with full benefits and a pension. She deserved it.

Chapter Five

~~~

T HE DAY AFTER THE FIRE AND the discovery of the murder victim, Detective Raymond Chen trudged up the hill towards Grace Church from police headquarters. He wasn't used to being winded, even on this twenty percent slope.

I need to ride my bike more. It's not an excuse to say I've been too busy with the headquarters job. And being too busy isn't a good enough excuse for not seeing Arlis.

He was climbing up the hill to see her now but hadn't called ahead or texted for fear she would hide out. It wasn't that they didn't get along. She was just such an introvert that it took about fifteen minutes of soft talk to calm her down. After Nick's murderer had been arrested, they'd gone out a few times, including to a Sunday service at Grace church and brunch after. But then she'd stopped answering his texts, and he got busy, and there they left it. Neither one of them was the type to fall suddenly and madly in love, so he had no idea how their relationship could go forward.

Stopping a block below the church to inhale again, he remembered what she'd told him during that brunch.

"Raymond, I've enjoyed today, but I'm sure you've figured out that I need a lot more alone space than most people."

He'd asked, "How much alone space?"

She'd moved her fingers up and down on the table, and he realized she was doing calculations.

"About 90% alone. But I'm trying to lower that to 80%"

"And how are you trying to do that?" he'd asked. He was afraid she wouldn't answer, but after a minute, she said,

"I probably should be seeing a therapist, or taking medication, but for now I'm having a weekly meeting with Deacon Mary. I really admire her, and she doesn't push me, and she has a wonderful husband and kids and grandkids. They've invited me for dinner and family holidays. I'm not saying I want a family like that, but I like thinking about it."

She continued, "And I'm doing something else, which is really suited to my personality. But I don't want to talk about it yet in case it doesn't work out."

"OK," he'd answered, "but could you just sum all this up in one of your French phrases?"

That had got her laughing.

"No, I can't. What I mean is that life is better, but not perfect."

HE GAINED THE SUMMIT and rounded the corner to the front door of the Old Rectory. Lester had told him about Arlis' involvement with the Central Seattle Message Board. That was probably the new activity she'd mentioned. Someone from the department would probably interview her about the message board, but he wanted to get her take on yesterday's events.

Would that be a violation of department rules or ethics? As he turned the knob on the Old Rectory's front door he decided, *not if I tell her I'm operating outside departmental boundaries but really want to get to the bottom of what's happening.* One thing he knew was that she would never get in the way of someone searching for the truth.

THE NEXT DAY, REV. Catherine and her guide dog Louette were waiting outside Father Robert's office when he arrived a bit later than usual. Still in post-honeymoon mode, he and Molly had enjoyed a leisurely waking up, a leisurely shared shower and a leisurely breakfast.

"Great to see you, partner," he said. "We have a meeting of the area clergy in one hour. I'll check my messages and then I'll drive us down to St. Columba's."

"No," she answered. "They're on the bus line. We'll catch the 7."

This was not the conversation she'd hoped to have with him this morning. She'd hoped to talk him into letting her stay until the end of the month, which would allow her the maximum income from the short-stay renters at her Olympia apartment. Then she'd return to her unpaid situations at the hospital and food bank and her occasional gigs filling in for vacationing clergy. When she wasn't drinking wine in the evening, she was more realistic.

Robert ushered her into his office, and they sat down. Both had coffee in hand, hers from McDonald's, his from Molly's plumbed in espresso machine.

"You mean the *Nut Run?*" he asked.

"So you've heard about it," she said, taking a deep sip of McDonald's best. "Yes, the Number 7, that specializes in transporting people to the hospital's mental health clinic. It's the way I get to most places I go in Seattle. Up the hill, there's groceries, and I can transfer for the arboretum and the lake. Downhill is the drugstore, the post office, the Pike Place Market, and—"

"I give, I give! That wasn't fair. But, really, Catherine, when you have the chance, isn't it nicer and more comfortable to go somewhere by car?"

"Not necessarily," she answered. "Especially when I'm with a bad driver. I can't see far enough to warn them, and I've participated in more than one fender bender."

Her fingers touched her watch. "I'm sure you're a fine driver, but I've heard about your ancient Rabbit and its sprung seats. The bus is leaving in five minutes and we'll reach St. Columba's just in time; can you humor me on this, Father?"

ONBOARD, SHE LOANED HIM some change, swiped her bus pass and they proceeded down the aisle—she and Louette walking, he careening, to the middle section.

"Rev. Catherine! Sit here, sit here! Who's your friend?" She waved a greeting and said, "Today we need to sit by Loren."

A man in his 30's looked up. On the crowded bus, the seat next to him was empty. It only took Robert a second to guess why. The seat was technically empty, but 95% of it was covered with sacks. The sacks seemed to be all filled with magazines.

Catherine stopped next to the seat. "Loren, this is my friend Robert. He'd like to sit next to you, so you'll have to rearrange things. And don't scowl; I can see that far. Robert here has a Mad magazine collection even bigger than yours."

Loren glanced at the balding man in a clerical collar.

"No way."

"Way." she answered. "Robert, sit down and talk to him. He collects lots of other magazines, but I think you'll find him almost as knowledgeable as you."

On the way back from the meeting, Robert thanked her for the introduction to Loren and then enthusiastically reported the interesting sights along the way.

"Oh, no! The old Brethren Church is being torn down. The sign says it's going to be a mixed-use development.

"My gosh, there's a Starbuck's where the jazz club used to be!"

A few blocks away from the Grace Church stop, he lamented, "and the public housing project, all those sweet shingled duplexes are gone! Catherine, I really am ashamed. I read that this was happening, but all I thought of was how the families living in the new mixed-use towers might come to church."

Catherine touched his arm. "I'll bet there's some history here."

"You're so right," he answered.

During and after the second world war, the national office of the Episcopal Church had created the category, or order, of deaconess, to help run the churches whose male priests were otherwise occupied in the military or other government service. The women received close to seminary-level training, often taught by professors from the male seminaries.

Many of the deaconesses married the returning clergy and couples were sent to what were then considered the mission fields of rural and Western America. In the 1950s, two of the single deaconesses landed at Grace Church, where they proceeded to recruit all the kids from the housing project into a thriving Sunday school and basketball team.

"So that's why we, I mean, the church has the old gym," said Catherine, as she rang the bell for their stop.

"Yea, as near as I can tell, the program fizzled out in the '60s, when the city stepped up with community centers and youth leagues. A few of those kids still come to church, and they make our best adult acolytes, because they were trained so well by those ladies. And one of the ladies is still with us, in her late eighties. I'll introduce you."

A series of rings from the mental health clients announced the hospital stop, also the stop for Grace Church. As Robert and Catherine walked the half block, he pointed out the other uses for which Grace Church's once-extensive property had been put to use: a public housing tower built in the '60s, the halfway house and the food bank.

BACK AT THE OFFICE, Catherine said, "Robert, I really need to talk to you about how long I'll be staying. I've let my Olympia apartment out until the end of the month. I don't expect any pay now that you're back, but if I could stay at the condo until then, it would really help. I have some fill-in work around South Puget Sound coming up, so I can—" Her voice trailed off. "I sound pretty desperate, don't I?"

Robert guided her to his sitting area but had to delay answering until he'd visited the restroom. The downside of a long, jerky bus ride.

"I have some good news. Back in a minute," he said, racing out of the office. He noticed that the men's continued to be used as a locker room by the many visitors to the church office. Washcloths, toothbrushes, and slivers of soap covered most every surface.

On his way back, he visited the tiny art gallery a few parishioners had created in an alcove and filled with items donated from their collections. His favorite was a statue of the Virgin Mary, originally designed for out-door placement.

His mind issued a bluster prayer, to the effect of, *Of course she could stay. In fact, if things worked out OK, she could stay at least until after Easter. And if he could get the congregation to increase their pledges, she could stay longer than that. And if he could ever make up his mind to retire, she could stay until his replacement was found. And if the Bishop told them she couldn't, why he'd—*

He touched Mary's face before returning to the office.

Catherine was seated with hands clasped, glasses off, eyes closed. He cleared his throat and took the other seat.

She opened her eyes and reached for her glasses.

"Don't bother to put them back on. I'm not much to look at. Catherine, friend, I can't bear to hear you beg for a place to stay. And what I really can't bear is for you to have to beg for a place as a minister of the church. I think that we can offer you a lot more than what you're asking."

"Father, that would be wonderful. I love it here. What, exactly?"

"It's Robert, remember, unless you want me to call you Reverend Catherine. You know that in the next year, Grace Church will need to decide what our mission will be in this part of the city. You know that it will involve decisions about property use, service to the community, and responsible financing of church operations. It will involve us in tons of planning, goal setting, prioritization; and it's making me sick just saying those words."

He rubbed his bald spot. "On top of your pastoral and preaching skills, you have the administrative know-how to help us make it happen. Look at how you've tackled all the nasty little projects I left for you. Poof! They're done!"

"That's pretty high praise," she answered, putting her glasses back on. "To be honest, a bit higher than my ability warrants. Yes, I do have administrative and pastoral skills, and I can negotiate the altar and all the stuff around it better than many who see better than I do. But I also have my limitations, chief among them a bluntness that puts off the more entitled church members and also the staff. You saw that on display yesterday when I lit into Terry and Henry for stalling on the fire prevention project."

Robert raised his hand.

"Just one more thing," she continued. "I'm also sort of a lone ranger. I never saw a committee I didn't want to run from, and I know the church is big on participatory decision making. You're a star in that area, according to just about everyone in the congregation."

"Don't you see?" he answered. "The two of us make the perfect team. Here's the deal, if you're willing to accept. Full salary and housing at the condo until the end of March. After that we'll ask for an increase in pledges and try to get grant funding for administration of our outreach programs."

Catherine bluntly asked, "Who's paying until March?"

"That's a secret," he answered, then changed the subject, saying, "The other thing we need to do right now is try to find out more about the body they found. I figure Lester will know the most."

"Let's talk to Arlis, too," added Catherine. "She seems to have mastered the online universe."

Chapter Six

~~~

THE THREE-STORY HOUSE ON SEATTLE'S FIRST Hill, a block above the Grace Church property, didn't draw much attention even though it was one of the few in the city still covered in environmentally taboo asbestos tiles. The house didn't have a style, although the Historical Society called it late Victorian. The rest of the block was lined with 1930s brick apartments and small storefronts intermixed with 21st century mixed use buildings.

307 Garfield was one of the few remaining historic houses on the hill above the freeway and had been built for a doctor and his family in 1898. The few others remaining included the Stimson-Green mansion occupied by the historical society, Grace Church's Old Rectory and a nearby Victorian converted to an antique shop. Since Garfield was a city-designated Green Street, the front of the old house had undergone façade greening. Two-story trellises purchased with grant funding were attached to the exterior and were covered in vines. None of them were blooming this time of year. Instead the historic structure was encased in what looked like shredded green wrapping paper.

In the 1960s, the city had planted Big Leaf Maples up and down the streets of First Hill, perhaps as mitigation for the noise from the new I-5 freeway. The trees were now too large for the narrow sidewalks, having now spread outward to invade the parking strips. The tree crowns were so intertwined with the overhead power lines that outages were common. Despite the inconvenience, the area's residents loved the leafy canopy and protested any attempt to remove their beloved maples, which now almost touched the ivy at 307 Garfield.

The sprawling house had been divided at some point into separate units with awkwardly placed entries, and the casual passerby would be hard pressed to know whether they were residential, commercial or both. Each entry had its own mailbox, labeled A, B, etc., but most also had a sign above the doorway with what seemed to be a last name, not a business name.

The lettering was faded, so presumably any business clients were of the long-term variety. Anyone trying to research the occupants would discover only that Olson, Berkshire and the others paid rent to the same out of state company called Fleetwood Holding.

AT 8 P.M. THE day after the jungle fire and discovery of the body, one window was lighted on the second-floor rear of 307 Garfield. Anyone looking up would be have seen a head that appeared to be hunched over a computer.

At 8:10, sitting in her apartment with her cat Voltaire on her lap, Arlis responded to her phone's ping and saw that a new comment had come into the Central Seattle message board. She took turns on evening moderator duties with the "dedicated staff."

The comment was at the end of the thread discussing the jungle fire and the discovery of the body. It seemed to respond to an earlier update giving the identity of the deceased but not the cause of death. She shivered as she read.

Poster #456 sounded crazy, vindictive and knew a bit too much about the circumstances of death. She needed help with this one. She started with Bill the scanner guy, even though he wasn't officially part of the Dedicated Staff.

"What do you make of this?" She forwarded the post, which ended, *You do realize this was just the start. Don't be surprised when the other infiltrators get the same treatment. That's just the law of the jungle, ha ha.*

Bill texted Arlis, Take it off the thread but keep evidence of the link somehow. Then park it somewhere safe. You'll figure it out; all I can do is work the scanner. Do you know any cops that are smart enough to handle this the right way?"

"*Oui*, I know someone, but I won't be able to reach him until morning." She'd been away from her office when Raymond visited and saw his card when she came back. She'd left it there and didn't have it in her to track him down tonight via the Department.

"You mean I shouldn't run it by the staff first?" she texted back.

"That's what I mean. Do you trust any of them to keep this to themselves? Another thing, this guy wants us to think it's one of the campers that did it. Just get hold of your contact first thing. It used to be I knew the id of every poster by the number, but I got into one too many scrapes with the nasty ones, and the staff changed the system. But I have my ways, Tee, hee-hee. I'll get to work on 456."

Arlis wasn't a great sleeper, and her best hours were between 5 and 8 a.m. At 8:15 the next morning, after she'd made a cup of tea and gone online, she found the second message. He (she knew it was he) had made it just under the wire. The board stopped accepting posts at 10 pm.

I posted in plenty of time; you're breaking the rules by not publishing it, even if you do the nanny delete thing. As you well know, all it takes is an extra click to read the deleted stuff. Don't try to outwit me. None of you are smart enough.

She race-walked the eight blocks from her apartment to the church and by 9:00 had Raymond on the line. He was fumbling with his coffee maker as they spoke. His shift didn't start until 2.

After listening the post, he merci'd her profusely then added, "I'm surprised he's using the Central Seattle board; it doesn't have that much of a following." Sensing the cold air coming over the line, he took a gulp of coffee and improvised, "but now that I think about it, it makes sense. Your part of town is the latest up and coming neighborhood, so he'd want everyone living near the jungle to know."

"So how should I proceed?" she asked. "One of our—contributors— thinks I should hide both the posts, so the site administrators don't interfere by jumping on the publicity."

Raymond was impressed. "You could pull that off? I can see you have a few things to teach me." He paused to turn a fresh pod into coffee. "I need to check with the brass; my only official role in this murder has been to guard the crime scene."

She answered, "He's sure to keep posting until someone other than me puts it online. Oh, I just remembered that Lester thinks the dead man was someone from the green streets group, maybe trying to infiltrate the forest to turn it into a hiking trail. Could that be true?"

"I doubt it. Why would this environmental guy want to trek through a muddy path a few feet away from a major interstate? And think about it. The so-called forest comes to a dead halt after four or five blocks. The only vegetation after that is underneath the I-90 connection, and then it's all weeds around the warehouse area."

"Maybe he didn't know that?"

"It's possible, but I'm not there. I'd better call this in."

Just then a blast of rain hit the window of Raymond's fourth-floor apartment in the International District. He hadn't succeeded in showing her his digs those few times they went out. Arlis believed in rendezvous-ing in third places, so she could make a quick escape if necessary. Did he really want to pursue a relationship with someone so high strung? But she was so smart about so many things and he'd come to know the woman with the big heart underneath the layers of scarfs and sweaters. She was also oblivious to cultural and class differences.

Arlis was watching the same squall fly up her street from the Southwest. "If you get permission to follow up, I can introduce you to my colleague and the rest of the staff. They might be able to help track him down."

"Arlis, that's awesome. I'll get back to you."

Jungle Murder Victim Belonged to Urban Forest Coalition

The stabbing victim found in a wooded area above Interstate 5 has been identified as thirty-two-year-old Patrick Taylor of Portland, OR. Mr. Taylor, the Northwest representative of the Urban Forest Coalition, was in Seattle to meet with the members of Green Streets Seattle. At the meeting, the two groups had agreed to collaborate on a project to link existing and future green streets to their respective cities' urban forests.

Members of the Seattle group speculate that Mr. Taylor may have been scouting access routes from the Garfield Avenue Green Street to the forested area called the jungle which lies to the East of the I-5 freeway. The steeply forested area is managed by the State Transportation Department and is home to a number of homeless persons.

Mr. Taylor was last seen at a coffee shop on the corner of Garfield and Madison Streets. His body was found in a clearing by firefighters respond-ing to a report of smoke. They found the remains of a small fire constructed of leaves and small tree limbs near the body. Police suspect that the body had been moved and that the fire was intended to draw their attention to the deceased. It was later revealed that cause of death was a knife wound which punctured the victim's lung.

The Green Streets Alliance plans a memorial march down Garfield Street and into the jungle (which they refer to as the central Seattle urban forest) starting at 10 a.m. on Saturday. They urge all supporters of re-greening and re-forestation to participate. They also plan to erect a memorial near the entrance to the forest which the victim used.

Representatives of the Seattle Homeless Coalition, headed by Gerry Stern, have vowed to block access to the forest area, calling the march an intrusion by gentrifiers into one of the few safe spaces available to marginalized citizens with nowhere else to go.

Representatives of the Green Streets/Urban Forest Coalition issued a statement in response: "We're not anti-homeless. Everybody needs a roof, and everybody needs a forest."

The article appeared in the Seattle Times and was also posted on the Central Seattle site where it soon had over 100 comments. The moderator of the day had deleted ten so far. Tempers were running high on both sides, and many of the commenters vociferously denounced both sides.

Clean up that jungle and clean it up now! If they won't work, boot them out of town.

Just goes to show that those tree-huggers have pine needles where their brains should be.

THE NEXT MORNING, DETECTIVE Raymond Chen was in his supervisor's office pitching for a role in the investigation of the jungle murder, as every media outlet in Seattle and beyond was describing it. He'd just shown Lieutenant Olson printouts from the Central Seattle website, highlighting the posts from #456. "This is either the bad guy or someone who's trying to mess with the investigation. And better yet, look at all the comments on *The Seattle Times'* article."

"I see," said the Lieutenant, getting up to refill his coffee cup.

Undaunted, Raymond continued, "If we can locate the original poster, which my contacts at the Central Seattle site say can be done, we'll get some good leads."

"You think so?" asked Bruce Olson.

Raymond answered, "Yes sir, I do. I can use the new technology fine. But I know that won't be enough. I may be young, but my parents and grandparents have taught me the value of the traditional methods. I've learned how to be respectful, to listen, to probe. Sir, if you would just give me a chance to help solve this murder, I promise to—"

"You're on," said the Lieutenant, "but remember, you're part of a team, whose other members may or may not support the values you express so sincerely. They also may not appreciate your associating with that ragtag crew from the church."

"But—"

"I expect you and the rest of the *official* team to keep me advised with one voice, at least daily but every five minutes as needed. And I expect that together you'll solve this thing."

He stood to usher Raymond out of the office but kept talking,

"I know as well as anyone that this case is raising issues that go way beyond the homeless jungle downtown and way beyond the Ballard I grew up in. Ballard today is full of car campers, parents with little kids no less, and the ordinary citizens there are pissed about it. They're also pissed that the streets are being taken over by outdoor tables and fountains and other things to trip over. Not to mention the silly-assed people who spend their time drinking coffee and protesting over every little thing, and you know what else?"

Fortunately, his phone rang, allowing Raymond to make his exit.

THE NEXT MORNING, RAYMOND met his team in the Department cafeteria. And boy, had Lieutenant Olson been right. Merilee, Ornette, and their lead Ben Collins were there early. He had to muscle a chair into the round table.

He stayed quiet while the others talked.

After five minutes it was obvious they weren't giving this case high priority, along the lines of *We'll poke around a little, and then put it to bed.* They must not have heard the Lieutenant's message.

He spoke up. "What do you want me to do? Since I'm the newbie, I can do the grunt work."

Silence

"Interview the family? Research the type of weapon? Look for witnesses?"

Silence.

"OK, I'll do that. Anything else?" He took the silence for assent.

Chapter Seven

~~~

Up the hill at Grace Church, Catherine was suggesting to Robert that they create a multi-pronged action plan addressing the development of their corner property.

"That's the same phrase the Bishop uses, but I won't hold it against you," said Robert, "so long as you do the preparing."

"Just tell me what you want to see happen and I'll translate it into action-speak."

"OK," he answered, "First, we're just down from a city-designated green street. It was torn up for six months while they created parking strip plantings and took out the parking spaces to make walking and cycling paths and those bulb outs that I keep running into." He saw the question in Catherine's eyes and added, "They're also called curb extensions."

"Oh, sure. They let Louette and me walk further out before being a target for cross traffic.

Robert smiled. "In that case, I won't complain about them anymore. I checked with the mayor's office this morning and the next step for Green Streets in this part of town is to add two or three mini-parks. The scary part here is that parking lots are the prime sites, being that they're eyesores and promote excessive single car use. But with a lot of jack hammering and artificial turf, voila! they can be turned into village greens.

"We've had a sweet deal for many years on our lot. The Creighton Brothers have let us use it for free when we have meetings during the week, and on Sundays when the commuters are kicking back at home.

They own at least half the lots in the city. Jack Creighton, senior was a member of Grace Church and is buried in the Memorial Garden. But I've heard the kids and grandkids want to sell out. That's bad news for Grace Church. We've sold or leased all our other property to support the half-way house and food bank. If Creighton lot number 15 is sold or donated for a mini park, we're in big trouble."

"Wait a sec while I get this down," said Catherine." And then I need to take Louette out to walk, pee and sniff. Someone else should have recommended a parking action plan a few years back."

Robert grabbed the new fleece lined jacket Molly had helped him select off the floor. He'd thrown it at the coat rack earlier but missed. "That would have been me, and right then it seemed more important to keep the church from falling down on our heads."

"Sorry boss. Now you've seen me in Action-Plan-Woman mode. What's the second problem you mentioned?"

Robert put on his new coat. "Let's get to that by walking over to the church parking lot."

As Robert, Catherine and Louette meandered down the street, he briefed her on the issue facing not only Grace Church, but also other historic buildings built in the late 1800s. It was a real miracle that their bricks, lath and plaster had lasted a through a whole century of deferred maintenance.

"And three earthquakes," he continued. "The big one in 1947, the tail end of the 1965 Alaska quake and last but not least the Ash Wednesday quake of 2002 that sent a chunk of the bell tower through the church's ceiling. That was before my time, but poor Father Ramsey was getting ready for Ash Wednesday services when the shaking started. The way he told it, there were doors to either side he could run towards. Luckily, he chose the right one."

Catherine answered, "I remember the '02 quake because we felt it in Olympia. The dome of the Capitol building and the bridge to the Westside were out of commission for months."

Circling the parking lot, they discussed how the suburban churches formed in the 1950s and well into the 2000s used impermeable but utilitarian materials, ensuring that maintenance would be minimal. And when maintenance was necessary, most were perfectly willing to incorporate low cost, unaesthetic fixes. In other words, for many, the glorious sanctuary or temple was no longer there to enhance the worship experience.

The people of Grace church were not standing for that, and they clung to its exterior Wilkinson stone, which had been mined in Washington State; and to the interior old growth fir walls and ceiling supports, and the German stained-glass windows and pipe organ. A bequest had covered the cost of repairing the bell tower, but nothing else.

Because of these sentiments, most of the parish was all in for developing the site of their Old Rectory and food bank into a mixed-use structure. The funds from the sale could be banked and used for repairs and maintenance.

The membership also knew that Seattle needed to create middle and low-income housing to meet demand. Prices of existing housing were soaring because of an influx of tech companies whose employees perched at the top end of the wage scale.

However, there was opposition, mostly outside the parish, consisting of longtime residents and historic preservationists who wanted to save every pre-1920 structure standing in the city. This included the rickety old Grace Church Rectory.

ON THE WAY BACK TO THE office, Robert and Catherine met Lester and his German Shepherd, Spike. Humans and dogs greeted each other, but one of the humans was not a happy camper.

"What's up, Lester?" asked Catherine.

"Are you feeling my vibes or something?" Lester growled. Spike watched his companion for a minute, then carefully put his paw on Lester's knee.

"You too, Spiko? You feel my vibes too?"

Spike raised his right paw to his master's upper arm. Unwittingly, he was following the protocol established for animal companions of humans suffering from ptsd.

Robert took in the fact that Lester's hair needed cutting, and that he was back to wearing his flannel shirt and greasy jeans instead of his sexton's uniform. He decided against confronting him on the street.

"See you tomorrow," he said. Tomorrow would be soon enough to talk to Lester.

ROBERT AND MOLLY ARRIVED HOME AT the same time. She asked him, "What happened to your new jacket? It's got a big dust streak down the back."

Robert shrugged. "I missed the coat rack. Hey Mol, remember we talked the other night about me taking a year or so to ease into retirement? With Catherine's help? I think I may have just started today, and it was great."

He took off his coat and was just about to throw it on the couch when a look from Molly sent him to the closet.

He called out over the rattle of hangers, "Catherine started working on an action plan to save our parking lot from turning into a park and then we started updating the proposal for developing the corner where the Old Rectory and food bank are now.

"Because she was helping there, I was able to plan for this Saturday's dueling marches, with the green street folks and the homeless coalition. I realized they'd be coming right by the church. So, I called the mayor's office and offered them the parish hall and church for—"

Molly interrupted, "Good for you. A gathering place for both sides. You and the mayor can talk them into marching together for both the homeless and the environment."

Robert frowned. "Actually, I offered the church as a communications and staging center. A place where government, law enforcement and the media could coordinate their activities."

"You offered a house of God for a staging center? It wouldn't have been good enough to hand out bottled water? Robert, if this is what pre-retirement means to you, count me out!"

Molly went into the den and closed the door. She hadn't felt so angry since—since when? She'd hardly been in the den since meeting Robert. It had been her deceased husband Jim's domain. Molly's eyes were drawn to a picture of Dr. James Ferguson receiving an award from the State Medical Association about twelve years earlier, just before his untimely death from a heart attack.

She stared at it for a full minute. Now her anger made sense. Jim had been a physician in a group practice. Well into his career he'd been blindsided by his partners, who turned the practice into what was called boutique medicine. Patients would pay a monthly fee to receive same day appointments, comprehensive testing, and access to the best specialists. No one on state assistance, or even Medicare, would be accepted. The patient, not the practice, would be responsible for seeking insurance reimbursement.

Jim had taken a financial loss to leave and become a sole practitioner, making himself available for referrals from community clinics. With his hospital affiliations, he'd been able to provide his patients with excellent care. And the Medical Association had recognized him with their humanitarian award. She realized that she was afraid that Robert wanted to turn Grace Parish into a boutique church, a church that would allow him to spend the last part of his ministry taking it easy in the company of the wealthy and well-connected.

When she came back to the living room, Robert was standing where she'd left him.

They stared at each other, and then he said, "What you said knocked the wind out of me."

"I've figured out what made me so angry," she answered. "Let's have some pre-dinner ice-cream out on the deck and I'll tell you."

Over mint chocolate chip for him and raspberry sorbet for her, Molly told him about her session in the library with Jim's picture. She added, "Now I realize it took a crisis for him to find his true calling."

Robert thought a minute and said, "And I've followed my calling from the beginning, but maybe the murders, and getting married to you, and this development project have pushed me off track. I seem to be getting caught up in a fantasy of being the big man on the block, hanging out with the mayor and big-time developers."

They knew that more conversation was needed but were both hungry now. "Help me put together a stir-fry," Molly said, "And we'll talk some more over a second helping of ice cream."

Chapter Eight

~~~

BILL THE SCANNER GUY SAT ON a surplus secretarial chair in the corner of his studio apartment. Because the bathroom was down the hall it qualified as an SRO, or Single Room Occupancy residence, one of the few remaining in Seattle.

He dozed off for a second and the liberated chair rolled across the off-kilter floor and banged against his neighbor's wall, the neighbor who worked the night shift and had just fallen asleep. Bill shouted an apology and rolled back to his computer, where he resumed writing his weekly essay for the Central Seattle website.

Publishing online essays indulged his need to express himself and were compensation for providing continuous monitoring of every radio frequency in the greater Seattle area for no pay. He survived on military benefits and his cheap rent.

During the interminable Gulf wars, he'd been a flight radio operator and had escaped injury. However, the tight quarters and a few falls had taken a toll on his back. After seven years in, he gratefully took full advantage of his VA benefits, including the commissary and the medical facilities at Joint Base Lewis McCord.

Before his back totally gave out, he'd overseen radio operations for some of the big Alaska fishing outfits based in Ballard. He'd also volunteered at every emergency command post that would have him and still provided communications advice to a variety of veteran-owned businesses. He would not answer to the word consultant.

Back in front of the screen, he deleted what he'd composed so far. Nobody told him what to write, because he stayed this side of libel and his reminiscences were popular with the site's readers. He had to be careful not to alienate the frequent posters, who provided the subscription dollars that kept the Central Seattle site alive.

He'd already finished his summary of the last three days' scanner reports. The summary was another service he insisted on providing, because he knew that at least half of the site's readers were too busy to log on every day. But just bury a post about two skateboarders getting it on two days ago and all hell broke loose.

He'd decided to focus this essay on the jungle murder, because the rest of the media had gone onto other things: today it was the Seahawks' chances this year. There wasn't much to report because the bombshell post from the other night had been suppressed, but Arlis had been feeding him tidbits from the detective she knew. He figured she was one of those introverted millennials who'd rather seek justice from behind the scenes.

He started again: "*Wednesday, Wednesday, hump day. You all may have moved on, but I just can't get that jungle murder off my mind. For instance, don't you think it's a bit much to kill a guy just because he wandered into the trees right next to a busy street, just down from the low-income housing tower, and just up from the freeway? Sure, he may have been what they call a green streets activist, but he'd just come here from Portland. Who would know him? And why was the place where he was murdered surrounded by trash, making it look like those filthy campers were responsible?*

"*I have another scenario in mind, being that this guy, carrying his designer coffee, was in the wrong place at the super wrong time and stumbled on something he shouldn't have. It reminds me of the time when I wandered into something bad after I left my so-called home at age thirteen.*"

He then recounted a harrowing yet heartwarming story from his youth. The post received 35 comments, all about his youthful adventures, none about the murder.

He wasn't going to give up. The next day he posted a notice about the march taking place on Saturday, which was again superseded by sports mania.

CATHERINE LEFT THE CHURCH AT 5. It was dusk, and the streetlights weren't casting much light.

"Take off your sunglasses, dear, and let's go," she told Louette, who shook herself and waited for the correct command. As they began the four-block walk to her condo, Catherine's thoughts turned to Lester. She was worried. It was out of character for him to be surly, and even she could see how disheveled he'd been. Robert had to go right into a meeting, but she knew he wasn't happy with the encounter either.

When she'd arrived at the church six weeks ago, Lester had put himself totally at her disposal, helping her move into the condo, taking her shopping, and providing extensive tours of the church grounds and neighborhood. He'd identified potential barriers and moved them. He'd helped her translate Daniel's speech. And dear Daniel was able to match the opening and closing hymns exactly to her pace to and from the altar.

Lester had warned her that the pigeons standing on 'bird lady Clare's' grave in the Memorial Garden weren't going anywhere, then told her about the events of two years ago that had caused Clare's death.

Passing the Old Rectory, she looked downhill to the left before allowing Louette to step off the curb. It was prudent to be careful here because the crossing was at the top of a twenty percent slope, which frightened even experienced drivers into rash actions, like ignoring the stop sign and barreling through, terrorizing pedestrians and cross traffic. Just as they stepped up the opposite curb by the halfway house, Louette came to an abrupt halt.

"Watch out!" came a voice to her left and a head appeared in front of her at waist level. It took a moment to realize that she'd almost collided with a man riding a mobility scooter.

"Well, how do you do?" he asked. "Sorry about that. I have a habit of gunning it at the top of this hill. That dog of yours is a champ, aren't you fella?"

Catherine slowly let her breath out. Their heads were about three feet apart, too close for her comfort.

"Her name is Louette. Would you mind moving ahead and we'll continue this conversation in front of the halfway house?"

"Ha! You're funny. Sure," he answered and executed a smooth turn to the left around the corner.

She followed and had Louette stop in front of the facility's office window where the security staff had their station. This fellow didn't set off any alarm signals, but you never knew.

Bill Bailey positioned his scooter off to the side facing the lady as she approached. He was intrigued. When was the last time he'd seen a woman in a clergy collared shirt wearing well-fitting jeans and narrow-toed Tony Lama boots?

After a few minutes' conversation, Catherine found herself intrigued by Bill's brash personality, his habit of not looking at you when he talked, his thick black and white hair, and his t-shirt with its large *So What?* logo.

He told her he'd never attended Grace Church, or any church, and waited to see how she'd react.

"How about Nick's Place?"

He answered, "Yea, I've been there. It's got a way better laundry than my dump. Don't worry, I put money in the donation box. I used to go over to the thrift shop to talk to Nick."

"You know what happened," she said.

"Yea. There aren't many things I regret in my life, but one of them is not preventing Nick's execution. I've known enough creeps like the guy who did it, and I should have realized why he was hanging out around here."

They talked easily for fifteen more minutes and then walked together to Madison St. Bill crossed; Catherine turned right.

Arlis looked out her office window and saw Rev. Catherine talking to a guy with a grey ponytail and riding a scooter. They were having an animated conversation. Something about him was familiar.

Chapter Nine

~~~

"IT'S WONDERFUL TO BE BACK WITH you all!" Father Robert, in clerical collar, gave what he hoped was an enthusiastic welcome to the group gathered on folding chairs in the parish hall. These people were what he thought of as his kitchen cabinet, the members of the parish and staff who could be counted on to provide him with spiritual straight talk and practical advice. They'd supported him through two deaths on the Grace Church property, one related to the failure of their crumbling bell tower, the other a straight-out murder.

Even though the tower was now standing tall, and Nick's murderer had confessed, he needed their help again.

To his right sat Dr. Lucy Lawrence, last year's senior warden, the key parish leader. This year's warden, Stacy Chase, was busy raising her baby but managed to conduct administrative business from her home office and nursery. Seated next to Dr. Lucy were Mary Martin, Grace Church's deacon, and Daniel LaSalle, Music Director, and organist. New this year was Reverend Catherine. He had been expecting a few others but decided to start on time.

"Before we begin, I'd like to offer a prayer," said Robert. "Unlike most of you, I'm not great at improvising, so I've chosen one from our book of Common Prayer called For Church Buildings and Institutions."

After the Amen, and before Robert could call the cabinet to order, Daniel stood up.

"Father, that was a good prayer, but I don't think it was the right one."

Except for Catherine, the rest of the group nodded.

Oh no. What was he missing?

Robert ventured, "Well, I want to talk about developing the corner of the Grace Church property to raise the money we need finish repairs on the church and parish hall. And then if we have time, I'd like to review Rev. Catherine's plan to make sure we don't lose our parking."

After a long pause, he continued, "But I guess that's not what you all had in mind."

Dr. Lucy spoke up.

"Father, I know we need to decide on those things, but don't you think our immediate challenge is to help find the person responsible for the murder of that poor young man?"

Daniel continued, "And Father, I know the murder didn't happen right on our own property, like the others. Ms. Clare was attacked in the Memorial Garden, and Mr. Nick was murdered in the Old Rectory, but I've been doing some reading about parish boundaries."

"You have?" asked Deacon Mary, the unofficial mentor for their beloved, but somewhat inarticulate musician.

Daniel rocked on his toes. "Yes, and now I know that our Grace Church boundaries start where we are right now and end halfway between us and the churches around us. So, I looked on Google Earth and saw that the place where Mr. Taylor was found is on our side of the boundary with St. Luke's to the South."

Robert felt like he was on another planet. *I don't have time to deal with this on top of the new development* .

Catherine half rose, in imitation of Daniel, who seemed to know how to get their attention. "Related to the murder, Deacon Mary and I did some checking and learned that Mr. Taylor's parents will be in town tomorrow. His body is being released the day after. Father, I hope it's OK, but we've made contact to see if they'd like some assistance from us."

Everyone nodded.

She continued, "We're waiting to hear if we can meet them at the airport and put them up in my condo's extra bedroom. It just seems like the right thing to do, and the Green Streets group their son met with before he was murdered don't seem to be reaching out. Their board had only met him once, and now they're involved in the dueling demonstrations planned for Saturday.

It was hard to know if she still had their attention, but she kept going.

"KORN TV sent Kate O'Reilly to Portland to interview the parents and she did her usual over the top sentimental thing. The poor couple was tongue tied. It's obvious they need support. As Daniel reminds us, we're the nearest church to where their son's body was found."

Father Robert rubbed his bald spot, took a breath, and asked, "Arlis?"

Following everyone else's lead, Arlis rose slightly and said, "I checked with Detective Chen to see if we could host the parents and he said it would be OK, as long as we kept them away from the politicians and media." The group noticed that her nondescript brown pageboy pulled back by bobby pins had been transformed into a tousled auburn mass streaked with blonde highlights.

Catherine re-entered the discussion. "So, Father, all you need to do is greet and pray with them if they want. Deacon Mary and I will accompany them to the morgue and any police interviews. We'll see if they want to come by the church to meet with the Green Streets people on the day of the march."

Robert confessed, "But I told the mayor's office that we'd be a communications command post for the demonstrations. The media and politicians will be right in their faces."

He faced another circle of questioning expressions.

"Didn't I tell you? Oh, I guess I told Molly, and she hated the idea."

In the silence his stomach growled. He and Molly had talked it out last night, but he'd left home before breakfast to make sure that their truce continued.

Daniel stood up again. "I have an idea. It's come to me all of a sudden. Here it is.

"We can put all the official people right here in the parish hall. I'll set up all the electronics. And then we can open up the church for the marchers who are tired or want to pray or talk to each other. The parents can sit away from the rest in the side chapel. Then we can put chairs out in the Memorial Garden for anyone who's afraid of church or have their dogs with them."

"Genius, Daniel!" said Catherine. The others nodded. "What do you think, Father Robert?" she asked.

He answered, "That's basically what Molly said I should do, try to get everyone communicating. We'll need to get the official buy-in."

"I'm on it," murmured Arlis, busy with her phone.

THE DOOR TO THE PARISH HALL screeched open on its unoiled hinges. Catherine spoke softly into her phone: *Silence parish hall door.*

"Sorry I'm late," shouted Ed Grafton. He ushered in two men and let the door slam behind them.

Ed was the head of a produce trucking company and on the board of the food bank. He also fancied himself as a property developer, but because Nick's murderer had almost succeeded in drawing him into his nefarious plans, Ed had a long way to go to gain the church's trust. To his credit, he'd discovered who was stealing donated supplies from the food bank and funneling them off to small convenience stores. He'd also donated a large sum to Father Robert's discretionary fund, used to help parishioners and other supplicants in dire financial straits.

Ed and crew walked up to the trestle table, which had no extra chairs.

Father Robert's brain screamed; *I have to eat before another meeting.* "Good to see you, Ed. Let's take a few minutes to set up another table." He sent an imploring look to Terry, one of Ed's companions.

Terry, the food bank director, knew that more was required than just a few extra chairs. "Hey all, it's lunchtime and we're in luck. The Trans-Pacific Hotel just brought by their whole lunch service. The client backed out at the last minute. The chicken almandine is still warm, and the food bank is closed for today. I say we use it to cater this meeting."

"Great," Robert rasped. "Let's meet back here in fifteen." He raced from the room to collapse in his office. He needed something to boost his blood sugar right then and found a protein bar in his desk drawer to hold him over.

Catherine looked up at the new fuzzy faces. "Welcome Mr. Grafton and Terry," and, to the third person, "you too. I guess we'll be introduced soon. Louette, do you need to go out? I sure do."

Arlis appeared at her side. "I'll take her out for you."

DETECTIVE RAYMOND CHEN WAS DRIVING UP the 20% grade next to the food bank when he spotted a woman with streaked auburn hair standing next to a black lab on the tiny strip of lawn.

Arlis jumped when she heard the screech of car brakes behind her. She turned around, trying not to entangle Louette's leash in her legs.

"*Bonjour*, Raymond," she said, patting the dog. 'This is Rev. Catherine's Labrador Louette. Isn't she adorable?"

He called through the lowered right window of his unmarked sedan,

"Sorry, I can't stop for conversation now. Except to compliment you on the hairstyle and say that I'm surprised to see you with a, a, I think it's a *chien*, rather than your, ah, *chat*."

"*Bien sur*, Raymond! I'm beginning to realize I must be an all-purpose animal lover. Especially this one, who is so well trained that she will only act like a playful *chien* when she is off her harness. Otherwise, all business!"

Cars were backing up behind Raymond, honking and revving their engines to avoid stalling out on the steep slope.

"Arlis, one more thing. You can't use me to relay information about the march coming up to the police chief and certainly not the mayor. Can I call you around seven tonight?"

"Yes, *oui*," she answered. "*Au revoir*."

THE LUNCH SERVICE IN THE PARISH hall included a mixed greens salad, chicken almandine, new potatoes, fresh asparagus from somewhere far away, rolls from a Seattle bakery, and a fruit and cheese plate. After everyone adjourned to use the facilities, catch a breath of air and check their messages, the meeting resumed.

The instant after Father Robert's Prayer for Church Institutions ended, Ed Grafton began talking.

"Father Robert, we might as well get this out of the way right now. It's not only the Old Rectory and the old gymnasium that have to go; it's also the Parish Hall, where we're sitting right now." He waved to the left. "The south wall next to the Memorial Garden can stay in some form, but this single-story space is taking up the vertical space we need for the project. None of the figures work out otherwise, isn't that right Andy?"

Andy, who'd accompanied Ed to the meeting, looked at his laptop and nodded.

Instead of going ballistic, Robert, relaxed after the meal, decided to remain silent. Catherine did too, following his lead.

Dr. Lucy, who'd just nibbled at the salad and chicken, asked, "Mr. Grafton, would you please introduce your associate?"

Grafton waved his hand to the right. "Oh, sure. This is Andy Fowler. Andy Fowler, Esq., to be exact. My attorney recommended him. Andy has an office up the hill and is handling a lot of the legal business for developers in this area. Isn't that right, Andy?"

Andy nodded but said no more. He was a short and solidly built figure in his light blue dress shirt and brown trousers. Above his square rimless glasses perched a puffy head of dark brown hair parted on the side, probably a hairpiece.

Robert said, "Ed, you're the best friend an ignorant church rector and vestry could have. You and Mr. Fowler appear to have formulated a plan that will attract the best developers and maximize the return to Grace Church. I'm sure you'll soon be presenting us with a full description of the project you have in mind. But before you get too far, tell me, what is your plan for accommodating the parking needs of the parish, as well as the residents of the grand facility you seem to be planning?"

Ed looked to his right where Andy Fowler, Esq. was punching keys.

When he hadn't spoken after half a minute, Ed answered.

"It's simple. Each unit will have the appropriate number of underground spaces according to whatever the city is requiring. The people who come on Sundays can use the surface parking you're already leasing."

After looking towards Robert and receiving a big nod, Catherine took over.

"I'm sorry to tell you this, Mr. Grafton, and Mr. Fowler, but it won't be quite as simple as that. Grace Church is busy every day of the week, with church services, the food bank, AA meetings and a lot else. And, sad to say, we may be losing our parking lease. We're not sure of the details, but Mr. Fowler might know."

Mr. Fowler wasn't saying, so Catherine turned her head toward Lucy, who picked the ball back up.

Even though her profession had been dentistry, Lucy had a head for business. For the next ten minutes, she and Ed Grafton bounced the ball back and forth, discussing the Grace Parish project scope, programmatic design, permitting, etc. She made it clear that whoever the developer turned out to be, project bidding and program management would be firmly in the church's court.

Ed had given up on Mr. Fowler and concluded the exchange by saying, "No matter how you decide to proceed, I'm on board. You probably don't know this, but I've managed to hang on to most of what I learned from my Methodist upbringing.

"True, I've had a few stumbles along the way, which you're all too aware of. The main takeaway for me is that it's possible to be successful and ethical at the same time. Although I have to say, it's a lot easier when the success comes first."

All eyes were turned towards him.

"Here's what I have to offer right now. There's space in one of my warehouses for the food bank, free, gratis, except for a nice tax write-off for my business."

Ed continued, "I don't care who ends up living in your new building, but I can assure you they're not going to put up with lines blocking the front door waiting for food and the rat-filled dumpsters next door. And Terry's told me that most of his clients—see, I'm learning the lingo—come from South of here, near my warehouse."

He stood up, motioning for Mr. Fowler to follow. "Get ahold of me when you want to meet again. Oh, by the way, I saw a sight for sore eyes on the way here. They're put up a big chain link fence around the entrance to the jungle, where that guy was murdered. The only way to get in or out now is from the freeway."

Mr. Fowler snapped down the lid of his laptop. "About time," he said.

AFTER ED GRAFTON AND MR. FOWLER were out of the building, Robert wondered out loud, "Where's Lester?"

"Yes, where's Lester?" they all repeated.

"I saw him going into the Old Rectory with Spike about 7 o'clock, last night, said Terry. "Maybe he's still asleep."

Chapter Ten

~~~

MOLLY FERGUSON VICKERS SAT AT THEIR kitchen table, idly watching the finches and sparrows attack the feeder she'd just filled. She and Robert had exchanged four texted apologies that day, each more heartfelt than the last.

They shared the house she'd built with her late husband Jim. The green streets being created all over the city were descendants of the graveled path below. She often waved to the walkers from the deck.

Her boss Bishop Anthony was preparing for retirement. His successor would be elected at the annual diocesan convention in three months. She would retire then and had an idea about how to fill her days.

Every year her women's club gave academic scholarships to deserving students, including older students. Volunteers from the club also provided career advice and donated clothing suitable for job interviews and the workplace. She'd donated many outfits over the years, especially as her own outfits became more casual. Now she'd start mentoring and raising scholarship funds.

She also wanted to be more involved at Grace Parish, so that she could deserve the title old Henry the Sexton had bestowed upon her: Rectorina.

WHEN RAYMOND GOT HOME THAT EVENING, the first thing he did after removing his shoes at the door was to phone Arlis. He hoped she would answer.

When she did, he jumped right in. "Driving by this afternoon, I couldn't help but notice the contrast between the new hairstyle and your uniform."

"My uniform?"

"You know, long grey sweater, jeans, birkies."

"Well," she replied, "I haven't decided how to proceed. Mother tricked me into the hairstyle."

He waited.

"She was treating me to a cut at her salon. I was sitting in a flimsy robe with my hair dripping wet when the stylist pulled out a paintbrush and started applying globs of colored stuff on parts of my hair."

He couldn't help saying, "Gee, I've always wanted to know how that was done."

"No, you haven't, she replied. "But if I decide to keep the multi-color effect, and that depends on Mother's willingness to pay, I'll consider continuing from the top down. Next would be to pluck my eyebrows, then invest in makeup, then the clothes, then the—"

Raymond interrupted, "One thing, and then we really need to get down to business. Please don't pluck away the little part of your eyebrows that look like ocean waves. Now I need to ask some questions about the jungle murder. First, where's Lester? I haven't been able to rouse him on the phone."

Despite the seriousness of the question, he would be happy to know that Arlis and her phone had walked to the bathroom mirror, where she was raising one eyebrow, then the other.

"You won't be able to," she answered, "because he left it on his bed along with the church keys. The last time anyone saw him was last night. He's gone to ground for some reason. Father Robert is worried he's trapped inside that fence you put up."

Raymond pounded on his kitchen counter, upsetting a carefully arranged vase of bamboo.

"Damn! Les was supposed to be helping me on this. Big help he'll be without a phone. He's probably joined up with his friend Ray from the Salish Center. He was worried we'd arrest him because he carries a carving knife."

His voice rose. "And it wasn't me or the police who put up that fence. The city is worried about those two marches coming up. They don't want the homeless advocates to get into a turf war with the green-streeters."

"Wait!" Arlis commanded. "I'm looking at a text saying there's been another murder! *Mon Dieu*, the body's hanging on the fence at the entrance to the jungle!"

Before disconnecting, Raymond yelled, "How do you find out about these things before anyone else!"

Father Robert had stayed late at church and heard the sirens. He turned on the radio and learned about the second murder. After whispering a prayer for the repose of the man's soul, he resumed worrying about Lester.

The note on his bed had said, 'Me and Spike are out of here. I took the steel toed boots but will reimburse you at a later time.' As was his custom, Lester summed up the situation by quoting the lyrics of a song, in this case mangling those of the Canadian musician Neil Young. *If I do come back later, I won't be back at all.*

Henry, the day sexton, had been furious. Thank God Daniel had offered to fill in tonight. For the time being, he was moving from the apartment he shared with his dad back to his old room at the rectory.

Like it or not, Robert realized, the development project would be on the back burner until the murders were solved and Lester was back.

As he trudged back to the parking lot, he remembered Daniel reminding them that the murder site was inside Grace Church's parish boundaries. He thought about what he'd seen on the bus ride with Catherine.

There was a time when Grace Church straddled the North and South parts of the city; the north better off, the south not so well-off. Now the dividing line of wealth was moving south, out of the central city.

However, their parish included the public hospital, the halfway house, the new, elegant condos and retirement centers, the public housing project, the people on the bus, the green street advocates, and the residents of the jungle. The opportunities for contact and cooperation were too precious to be lost. He'd reassemble his original team in the morning.

After getting home to Molly, he needed to make two—no, three phone calls.

Chapter Eleven

$\sim\!\sim$

THE SECOND VICTIM WAS A FILIPINO man in his forties who'd been killed by a gunshot wound to the chest and then tied by the wrists to the outside of the newly erected fence enclosing the jungle. The hospital employee who discovered the body on her way down the hill was horrified. So was Raymond when he joined the responding officer.

The wallet in the victim's jeans made identification easy. A records check showed that Daniel Ramos was a casual laborer who worked mostly around the docks and rented a room in the industrial area South of downtown. His rap sheet wasn't long, listing arrests for misdemeanor theft and possession of marijuana.

THIRTY MINUTES LATER, DETECTIVE DAVE JOHNSON, the senior member of Raymond's team, arrived. how did you get here so soon?" "Is it because you live in the International District?"

"Well, it wasn't because you or one of the team let me know. Yeah, Dave," Raymond said, "I live in the hood. No worries, though. Your hood is Shoreline. Not so many murders there. But if you'd been listening to the scanner, you'd have been here sooner."

"No thanks," Dave answered. "I'd rather put my kids to bed without scanner talk in the background."

"You've got a point. Anyway," Raymond continued, "I've got officers over at the public housing tower finding out if anyone was looking down here when Mr. Ramos was chained to the fence. It seems like the murder happened somewhere else, just like with Mr. Taylor."

They both stared up at the multi-story concrete building built in the last days of federally funded housing dedicated to low income residents, mostly elderly or disabled.

Raymond tried to work the mental muscles he'd developed at the University of Washington. He noted the "brutalist" style of architecture but appreciated the concrete striping and vertical windows and how well maintained it all seemed. He remembered that the church's beloved parishioner Mae had lived there.

"What else?" his fellow detective prodded.

"The other thing that's happened was Mr. Taylor's parents came into town today and told Bart that their son was a nature freak and a real nerd. The parent are staying at a condo the church owns.

"Thanks, bro," said Detective Dave. "I've been off for a few days. Bart covered for me. And—I guess you didn't know that."

"No worries," answered Raymond, "I'm the newbie. I just hope I jump through all the hoops correctly, so I can get your job when you're promoted."

Just then, Mr. Ramos' body was carried away, and both detectives stood at attention until the ambulance drove around the corner.

It took a full two days after Mr. Ramos' murder for Father Robert to regather his kitchen cabinet. Thank God the city had withdrawn the permits for the dueling street marches scheduled for that Saturday. Neither the Green Streets Alliance or the Homeless Rights Coalition had objected.

At 10 a.m. on Friday, the meeting began. As usual, it was held in the Parish hall, which was too large, the problem being that every other space at the church was too small.

"Thank you all for coming," Robert said. He wore a clergy shirt, khakis, and polished brown loafers.

"Most of you know that I start meetings here at the church with a prayer. Today, we'll do intercessory prayer, meaning asking God's help for people who need it. I'll start by asking for special prayers for Lester, our night sexton. Lester's also our emissary to the homeless community, which he was part of until last year, and now he's missing. Please, God, keep him and his dog Spike under your care and bring them back to us safely."

He choked, prompting tears all around.

Daniel, the church's musician, went next. "I'm praying for Lester and Spike and the two people who have died. And for the homeless forest campers and the environmentalists that they try to get along with each other."

Lucy Lawrence, again substituting for Stacy Chase, had been present during the earlier two deaths at the parish, the second a cold-blooded murder. "I'm also praying for Lester and Spike. I think Les is trying to find out who murdered Mr. Taylor and now Mr. Ramos. I can only guess that he's trying to prove that someone other than a homeless person or his friend Pete is responsible. In any case, there's a murderer out there. Frankly, I haven't thought it was wise for us to be so involved, but I also admit I felt that way about the other two deaths. But somehow, our little band was able to help the police both times."

Everyone waited a full minute while she decided what to say next.

"I'm near the end of my life, and I want it to be the best life it can be until its end." She cleared her throat. "My faith has been supported by this church for many years and Grace Church has also surrounded me with a loving community. To use the current term, count me in."

Catherine, wiping her eyes, patted Louette and added, "In addition to what's been said, please pray for a man named Bill I met in the neighborhood the other day. He needs an accessible place to live because he's in a wheelchair. He earns just enough not to qualify for low income housing but not enough to afford a decent place. I'm going to propose that we include a large percentage of accessible units when we develop our corner property."

Arlis snapped to attention at the name Bill. Bill was the name of the self-titled Scanner Guy for the Central Seattle website, who she'd suspected was housebound. She had no idea where he lived but remembered that yesterday she had looked out her office window and saw Rev. Catherine talking to a man on a mobility scooter.

They were all waiting for her prayer. She took the long deep breath recommended by the ancients as well as Deacon Mary in such a situation. For good measure she tapped her hands right and left, right and left, on her knees. She'd learned that from her current therapist.

She then addressed the group with a long string of French words, which roughly translated to *My God, help me not to faint*. None of them spoke French, but they knew her preference for the language and recognized the word *Dieu*, and so accepted her prayer in the spirit she wished she had intended.

Robert took a deep breath. "Now I'll introduce our guests." His volunteer assistant Adele had provided him with the names and a bit of biographical information based on the request he'd sent her. "To my left is Gerry Stern, who heads the Seattle Homeless Rights Coalition. To his left is Murph, who prefers to go by his first name. Murph, I understand that you call the nearby forest your home."

Gerry, a man in his early 40's dressed in jeans, khaki shirt, steel-toed work boots and green canvas coat, waved to the group. Murph, dressed in decrepit jeans, unfashionable tennis shoes and a heavy hooded sweatshirt, nodded.

Robert continued, "And to my right is Barry Larsen, Executive Director of the Seattle Green Streets Alliance."

Barry stood up. He wore a fleece lined parka, the type of expedition pants sold by REI, and lace up hiking boots.

Robert motioned him to sit. "Before you make your presentations, have any of you seen Lester?"

Barry half rose and answered, "Sorry, I haven't. I don't live in this part of town and as you know," he turned toward Mr. Stern, "our members aren't welcome in the forest."

Mr. Stern answered, "Maybe that's because it isn't a forest. It's a freeway buffer owned by the State Department of Transportation, commonly known as the jungle. And if your Alliance folks want to embark on expeditions into the jungle, I'm sure for a small fee I can arrange for Murph and his friends to escort you. And no, I haven't seen Lester."

Robert intervened. "Murph, have you seen Lester?"

Murph moved his head slightly in what could have been a yes or a no.

Robert turned to Gerry. "Since you've begun, go ahead. But I want Murph to get equal time."

Murph shrugged and withdrew further into his hood.

Robert said, "No need to talk. Nodding and whatnot will do fine.

"All right, Gerry, continue, but please start by telling us how you got to be head of the Coalition."

Gerry didn't seem pleased but answered, "After I dropped out of university, I enrolled in a welding program and got my certification. Then the union hired me as an organizer, but after that the Free Trade Agreement busted the unions. So, I bounced around getting work where

I could, and when a lot of my work buddies were living on the streets, I started the Coalition. That's it."

Daniel, rocking back and forth as he did except when playing the organ, asked, "And please, can I ask where both of you live?"

Gerry seemed eager to answer. "In an old boarding house on Industrial Way with some other organizers."

Barry hesitated, and then answered, "I live East of here with my wife and two kids."

Gerry wasted no time. "Oh, you mean Madison Park, average home price $800,000?"

Robert took his turn. "Full Disclosure. I live with my wife in a forested area a half mile above Lake Washington. Before I married, I lived next door in the Old Rectory, a block above the freeway, with bars on the windows. Then I lived in a condo left to us by a member of the parish. And I was happy in both places. You know, we all live where our circumstances allow. I could go on, but let's get back to life in the forest, or jungle, if you prefer."

"To get to the point," said Gerry, "anyone who visits the jungle isn't going to like what they see. Obviously the two dead men didn't. They ran into the kind of people who would murder someone for no reason. And Barry, your members aren't going to encounter any pretty birds. What robin, or even crow, wants to live next to a noisy freeway?"

He pointed to a canvas bag at his feet. "I've got all the stats on decibels for you to look at later. Even the bushes and trees are ugly. People who need to keep warm rip branches off for firewood. Not to mention the piles of garbage which the media love to describe in gory detail. Too bad they haven't figured out that every other Seattle neighborhood is outfitted with cans and dumpsters. "

Murph nodded.

Gerry continued, "Not to mention the piss and poop, which I'm sure Murph wishes could go in latrines instead of on the ground.

Dr. Lucy interrupted, "I'm sure that our current warden, if she weren't on maternity leave, would say that we'll supply dumpsters, latrines and washing stations."

Gerry halted.

"Be careful what you wish for at Grace Church," said Dr. Lucy. "You may just get it." She continued, "And along this vein, I'll bet Murph here would appreciate some attention for his aches and pains but is a bit fearful about making it down the hill to the free clinic. Maybe he tried once or twice and found a line going around the block."

Vigorous nodding under his hood.

"What if the medical folks came to him. And if he needed a clinic or a hospital—"

"Wait a minute," interrupted Barry . He stood up and looked for a non-existent podium.

"The things you're talking about are great, but shouldn't there be better places to live than a steep hillside above the freeway? Even our group doesn't advocate the forest as a destination, just part of a connector route between neighborhoods and parks. But we do have access to funds to create a few trails, maybe even enough to bridge the ravine near I-90. Of course, none of this seems likely now that one of our colleagues was murdered for the unpardonable offense of venturing a few hundred yards into the forest."

"Remember" said Robert, "we don't know where he was murdered, or why, or by whom."

The parish hall's steam heat had finally kicked in, with loud banging noises. Barry took a minute to extricate himself from his jacket.

"The message is the same. Anyone other than homeless aren't welcome. And forgive me, but if Murph and his friends can make it down to the freeway to panhandle, couldn't they make it a few more blocks to the clinics?"

Gerry craned his neck around the room. Ignoring Barry's last question, he asked, "Where are these better living places you mentioned awhile back?"

He continued, "I'll bet Murph here has tried them all. Maybe he started at the Gospel Mission, where it's so crowded you have to sleep on top of each other. Maybe then he found one of the tent cities that move from parking lot to parking lot, all of which seem to flood in the winter.

And Father, I know your church basement rotates with other churches for overnights. But think about it. Where's Murph going to store his tarp, his bedding and clothes in the meantime?"

Dr. Lucy answered, "Stacy would say that we'll supply storage lockers."

Gerry continued, "Then Murph tried underneath the bridges near the waterfront, where the druggies love to set fires and raise other hell."

His phone released the sound of a siren, which Gerry ignored but chose not to silence.

"And Barry, there already are trails, maybe not as nice as what you have in mind. They're near where your colleague was found, and I'm sorry that happened. The main one starts as a utility road below the hospital and winds up to Aguilar Park."

He chuckled. "I can just picture it. Murph and his buddies dragging their possessions from one place to the other after being busted. And then run off the road by your trailblazers headed to the park to put in solar lights and add some native plants.

"To wrap this up, after being preached at, harassed, robbed, beat up and generally treated like dirt, Murph tries to find a bit of peace in the jungle, which will end when he has to share the road with your weekend warriors."

Robert leaned forward. "Gerry, these two murders have ended the peace."

Daniel had moved from his chair to the piano and was playing the peaceful music he'd chosen. For a minute, everyone listened.

Robert asked, "Can we agree that everyone deserves a safe, dry, sanitary place to sleep no matter if it's indoors or out, tent, car, room, whatever."

Nods all around.

He continued, "And that the area above the freeway is our parish here at Grace Church?"

"And that everyone needs a place to hang out, like at Nick's Place in our Old Rectory," added Rev. Catherine.

Everyone nodded.

Barry jumped in. "And can we agree that trees, green spaces, safe paths and trails belong not only in the country but also in the city? And that homeless need housing that's permanent and provides the necessary services?"

Nods all around, except for Gerry Stern.

Lucy followed, "And that people living in their cars or RV's need a safe place too?"

Everyone nodded.

"Good," said Robert. "Adele's been taking notes and has offered to create a display here in the parish hall." He stood, and added, "Thank you for coming," , to forestall additional comments. "We're looking forward to hosting both of your groups again. We'll also invite reps from the city and police to answer questions about the murder investigations and their plans to create safe housing for everyone. It's a tall order, and I hope and pray we all live up to it."

Gerry hurried out, forgetting his acoustic charts. Barry Larsen walked out to the Memorial Garden, where Robert joined him. The Rhodies weren't in bloom, but the grass was a brilliant green and a bright yellow-blooming winter jasmine ascended the West wall.

"Father, this would make a great pocket park. Our group could add a gravel path around the edges and put in some seating, maybe a few tables for eating and chess matches. In nice weather, we could arrange for a couple of food trucks." He looked at the narrow street fronting the church. "You know, this whole area should be cordoned off."

Robert suppressed a chuckle. "Well actually, this space already hosts many souls, residing underneath the turf. We call it our Memorial Garden. Our dearly departed don't mind sharing the space, but Mae just to our left may not want a game table on top of her. And you notice the pigeons in the corner. That's where their benefactor Clare is resting. I'm afraid they have dibs on that space."

Robert pointed. "And see these cast concrete benches scattered around the perimeter? They were all donated by the deceaseds family members. The people in our neighborhood already use them to eat lunch, visit and meditate. And on special occasions, our departed host Easter Egg hunts and St. Francis Day animal blessings. You see, this Memorial Garden is doing just what your group wants, just a bit more traditionally. I hope you agree."

AS THE MEETING WAS BREAKING UP, Daniel walked to a workstation that had been set up outside the circle of chairs by Father Robert's assistant Adele Evans.

"Mrs. Evans, I didn't know you were here. I'm sorry for not noticing. I was too interested in making this a peaceful place by playing the piano."

"Th, thank you for noticing at all," said Mrs. Evans.

Daniel asked, "Can I see what's on your screen? And here's Father Robert and Rev. Catherine. Can they see it too?"

"Of course." She moved aside to show them what looked like a bird's eye view of the area around Grace Church. The church and its grounds were roughly in the middle, surrounded by the low and high-income housing towers, the hospital, the jungle, and the parking lots to the North. The Salish Center and Aguilar Park were at the Southern end.

An RIP marked the sites where the bodies were found, one near the Eastern end, the other at the North end two blocks over from Grace Church. A few tents were set among the trees. Tiny figures waited in line for the food bank.

The rendering was colorful and charming.

"Mrs. Evans, that's beautiful," said Daniel. "I'm not surprised that you created this, because when you were in charge of the thrift shop, it looked like a fancy department store."

"Look at all the paths," said Robert, who'd returned from his conversation with Mr. Larsen. "Some of them seem to start above the freeway and take up again on the lower side. I wonder what that's about? And look, there are the chain link fences and the roads for work trucks."

Daniel took up the narrative. "And there's the path that Mr. Stern talked about going to Aguilar Park. Mrs. Evans, this is like a symphony!"

"I agree," said Robert. "Adele, how did you do this?"

Adele ducked her head and pushed a stray hair into place.

"Y-you can find much of the information online, including apps to create a specialized map. I phoned some city offices and met with Murph before the meeting. He's been here a few times for bus vouchers."

Robert waved his arms. "You invited Murph to the meeting? I thought he came with Gerry Stern."

Dr. Lucy had joined the group. "I was just talking to Murph about his situation. In the meeting when we were talking about sanitation, he whispered the word *needles*. I followed him out and asked how big a problem drug use was in the forest. All he would say was, 'Not the way you think.' He agreed to meet me here tomorrow and I'll take him to the clinic. Did you notice his limp? He has a big sore on his leg. I'll see what else I can find out."

Robert said, "And the other thing we're going to do is forward everything we learn to Detective Chen. And we'll do it through me."

Lucy hesitated slightly. Father Robert wasn't known for giving directives. "Of course, Father, I'll let you know."

Catherine added, "I'll work with Adele to create a wall display, including the goals we discussed. Then we'll run it by you."

Chapter Twelve

~~~

ROBERT WASN'T SURE WHY HE'D KEPT the 1985 Rabbit Diesel so long. It was his only takeaway from the ancient history of his divorce, but it wasn't sentiment that kept him in the scruffy driver's seat. Years of living in shabby rectories on a relatively small salary had reinforced his natural cheapness, and he'd never tired of using the manual transmission. Since his marriage to Molly, his economic circumstances had improved, and he'd come to realize that the car was on its last legs.

"Robert, I know you love Rabbit," Molly told him, "so I won't insist you get a new car. However, when we go anywhere together, it will be in Red," the name of her late model convertible.

Today was the moment of truth. He pulled out of the church parking lot, turned down the steep grade and coasted under the freeway. He downshifted to second as he made a left turn and chugged back up towards the International District. Rabbit belched a puff of smoke with that unmistakable diesel smell.

He was traveling to Leon's German Auto Repair to have the transmission looked at. Leon had warned him over the phone that replacements were almost impossible to find.

Driving down Industrial Way towards Leon's, Robert glanced at the warehouses and wholesale outlets and remembered that Gerry Stern of the Homeless Coalition said he lived on Industrial Way. His place was probably further South near Boeing Field, where there was a small cluster of 1940s era boarding houses and apartments used by aircraft workers in WW2.

After the meeting he and Adele had looked up Gerry's group and Barry Larsen's Green Streets Alliance. Green Streets was part of a West coast-based group that seemed to enjoy substantial foundation funding. According to Adele, their Yelp rating was 4 ½, whatever that meant.

The Homeless Coalition was more modest. Its webpage was heavy on pictures from various marches and demonstrations. The marchers didn't wear bandanas over their mouths like the anarchist groups but had the same ragged appearance. He didn't see a single black or brown face.

None of these groups would be going away. Grace Church would have to work not only with the advocates of green streets and homeless rights but also the historic preservation groups and the downtown developers as they planned the future of their corner property.

A stalled car loomed in front of him and he slammed on the brakes. Thank God he'd had them replaced last year.

TWO PEOPLE STOOD OUTSIDE IN THE narrow doorway on the back side of Grace Church. The structure loomed like a stone fortress above the sloping street. The door was padlocked and the only other break in the wall was a stained-glass window high above. Cars, trucks and busses hurtled down the hill a few feet away.

After five minutes conversation, one of the two crossed the street towards the public housing tower. The other person headed up what used to be called "Profanity Hill." One hundred years earlier, people too poor to afford the streetcar uttered any number of oaths as they trudged up towards the city's original courthouse, located at the very top.

Grace Church in those days provided a water spigot and a chained tin cup for the thirsty travelers. Rumor had it that the pipe was fed by an underground spring. Now, the only vestige of this charitable gesture was a niche carved into the Wilkinson stone-clad wall, much like one that would hold a religious statue. These days, it held a wide variety of objects, the most common being empty water bottles, but sometimes there was one of the few remaining flowers from the street side planters, an unsuccessful attempt to beautify the area.

A block above the church, the incline lessened somewhat, passing along a retaining wall clad in the same Wilkinson stone as the church. The person entered the side door of an old Victorian home now divided into multiple units. The door slammed shut behind him.

"Molly, can you come get me? The verdict's in on the transmission and I've said goodbye to Rabbit. Leon's going to break it down for parts, so its spirit will live on."

"Sorry, I can't, dear. I'm up to my eyebrows sorting clothing donations for the Dress for Success program. You'll have to call for a ride."

Industrial Way traffic was long on delivery vans and tanker trucks and short on taxis and the type of sedan used by ride hire services. He hesitated. "OK, I can do that."

A number 6 bus whizzed by heading South, as he was getting ready to call for a ride, and he noticed the inbound stop across the street. The next crosswalk was two blocks away and he began walking towards it. No way was he going to jaywalk across six lanes of vehicles twice as tall as he was.

He'd barely made it when the inbound bus pulled up. He didn't have a Bus Pass and wasn't sure he had enough in his pocket for the fare. The driver motioned him to the side while the better prepared riders paid with the correct change or tapped their cards. Robert managed to locate the correct amount but when the patient driver asked if he needed a transfer, he didn't know, so he said yes. He was too intimidated to bother the driver by asking where the Number 6 was taking them, but his friendly seat mate assured him it would be within two blocks of the church—two uphill blocks.

He really didn't need to go back to the church, so he asked if his transfer pass could take him towards Lake Washington. It could. Five minutes after his transfer stop, he was home.

At dinner he asked Molly, "Do you think we could manage with just one car? On nice days, it's a 20-minute walk to church. I can get a bus pass to travel around town. Don't you think it would set a good example for the parish for us to be a one car household?"

"Yes, it would, she answered, "but I've noticed that trying to set a good example can backfire. Remember when Bishop Anthony decided to follow the food bank diet along with Terry? After ten days without sugar he'd offended so many people that his wife begged us to make him stop."

Robert laughed. "Remember, Terry and I called a halt to the diet and gave the Bishop a commendation. How about we try one car for two weeks and see what happens?"

"OK dear, as long as you remember that I get first dibs on our only car."

Chapter Thirteen

~~~

IT WAS ROBERT'S FIRST SUNDAY SINCE returning from his honeymoon. He hummed the old cowboy tune *Back in the Saddle Again* as he and Catherine set up the altar for the Communion Service. This was usually deacon Mary's job, but she'd been summoned by the Bishop to assist at a Cathedral event.

"Mary always calls what we're doing setting the table," he whispered, since there were a few early birds in the pews.

"Love it," she whispered back. "You're lucky to have a deacon. All of my postings have had me doing everything from unlocking the church doors to cleaning up after coffee hour."

Robert picked up a flower that had floated away from its vase near the altar. Then he watched a few more worshippers take their seats.

"I'll tell you what else is different. Look what they're carrying."

She raised an eyebrow over her thick lenses.

"Scratch that. I'll tell you. Ten years ago, even these millennials would have been carrying a prayer book. Now it's a coffee cup in one hand and a phone in the other. They probably want to catch up on emails or check the sports scores before the service starts. Their elders stay in the parish hall until the last minute, visiting in person with their friends."

He stifled a laugh. "They see us watching. They're hiding coffee cups on the floor and stuffing phones into their purses and pockets."

Because the sanctuary was relatively empty and no one was on their knees in prayer, he called out, "Don't worry; we're happy you're here. All

I ask is that you don't rate my sermon performance on Yelp until I have a few more Sundays under my belt."

His sermon was based on one he and Molly had heard in California during their honeymoon. He gave the preacher full credit since plagiarism is equivalent to a mortal sin in today's churches.

"Why are we here this fine Fall Sunday morning?" Robert began. "After all, the Seahawks are playing, and the weather's nice for a change. And I don't just mean you, I mean me too, and Rev. Catherine and her guide dog Louette, who'd rather be taking a nice walk." Louette, curled up next to the organ near her friend Daniel, barely raised an ear.

"I'll tell you why I'm here. To put it inelegantly, church on Sunday keeps me from running off the rails. Let me explain the railroad metaphor. Molly and I visited my hometown of Livingston, Montana on our honeymoon and ever since I've been thinking about my childhood. I loved trains when I was growing up. There were more train stations than airports in the '50s and '60s, and our Montana towns were strung out along the tracks.

"When you needed to go to Spokane for a hospital test or to Great Falls to buy Christmas presents, you caught the train, sometimes in the middle of the night in the middle of a blizzard. Watching the huge light coming towards you down the tracks and hearing the wail of the whistle was otherworldly.

"When I was ten, my parents gave me a Lionel train-set for Christmas. It ran all around the Christmas tree with me at the controls. They had to drag me out to Midnight Mass that year."

He waited for a bit while the older members of the congregation reminisced with each other in whispers. The millennials were sneaking glances at their phones.

"Those of you younger than 45 can substitute race cars or speed boats if you want. "We know what a tragedy it can be when trains derail or a car goes off a cliff or a boat runs aground. Just think about the train that jumped the tracks on the bridge south of Tacoma. Some of the cars fell onto the freeway and others dangled over the bridge. Passengers who escaped through the windows found themselves hanging off the bushes because the hill was so steep." He looked out and noticed the wide eyes of some in the congregation. Maybe the image had been too vivid.

"When these tragedies happen, sometimes it's because the operator is inexperienced or hasn't been paying attention or there's some sort of equipment malfunction. My toy train suffered this fate many times, usually when I left the controls to get a cookie from the kitchen.

"The fact is, we humans, despite eons of evolution, tend to run off the rails at the barest hint of a threat. What I mean is that we revert to survival mode. We call it fight or flight. The only person I know of who didn't lived 2000 years ago and was way ahead of his time. And even he got lots of guidance from his Father.

"Most of these survival instincts aren't pretty. Think Cain and Abel, David and Goliath. Our ancestors did their best to contain them, calling them the deadly sins, the Thou Shalt Nots, the Ten Commandments. We see lots of examples today, like—"

"Road rage," called out Henry from the third row.

"Greed," said another.

"Indifference," added Lucy.

"Thanks for the help," Robert said.

"So how do we stay on the track that our Savior has laid down for us? How do we get the best of the devils? Here's what I think is crucial, which I learned from the preacher in California. At this point in our growth as a species, we need to be nudged, not bludgeoned, to better behavior. Most of us are beyond the point where shaming, browbeating, or threats of hell will work.

"And nudging comes best in small increments, about once a week."

He paused long enough to focus everyone's attention.

"We've had four people die on our church grounds or within a few blocks in the past three years. The first was our friend Clare. She'd been an East coast socialite but succumbed to mental illness, found her way to Seattle, and developed a fixation on birds, specifically pigeons. Remember her wearing that long brown robe and the pigeons following her wherever she went? Her favorite place seemed to be our Memorial Garden. And remember she died after someone pushed off the rails by insecurity and greed dropped a stone off the church tower, which fell on her head."

Many in the congregation sighed and murmured to each other. They remembered the huge display of flowers and bags of birdseed left in the garden as a memorial.

Robert continued, "Then last year our parishioner Nick Monte was murdered by a person whom he'd loved as a substitute father."

Nick had been viewed as something of a saint at Grace Church, and many eyes were wiped.

"And now we have two more violent deaths in our neighborhood. We don't know the motivation behind these crimes, but you can be sure it wasn't charity. These four deaths I've described are reminders of the worst that happens when people go off the rails. We also need to include in this train wreck homelessness, poverty, addiction and violence. In our parish, unlike some others, they co-exist with well-funded hospitals, art museums and high-rise condos."

Robert could have said more, but his stamina was gone.

He concluded, "I like to think that Grace Church has served as a safe place during all this, but Grace Church won't keep standing unless we find the money to keep it upright and stable.

"What do we do? Dedicate our property for low income housing, or cut back the square feet to allow for the wide path that the Green Street proponents would like? Or sell to a condo developer for more money and continue to gentrify the area, pushing the problems in another direction? Or is there an alternative that will keep Grace Church on track both financially and spiritually?

"My prayer today is that together we welcome our Sunday nudges, stay safely on the track and follow it home. Amen."

"Amen," they answered.

SHAKING HANDS AFTER THE SERVICE, ROBERT was surprised to see Barry Larsen from the Green Streets Coalition with his wife and two children. Mr. Larsen gave him a thumbs up, mouthed "soccer practice" and hurried out.

After the service and an infusion of coffee and cookies, Robert held a forum in the parish hall. First, he announced that Rev. Catherine's salary had been funded by an anonymous donor for the next six months. This received sustained applause.

"It's not that we don't love you, Father Robert," said 75-year-old Marty Wilson. "But she's such an inspiration to the women of this parish."

"How about the men?" yelled Henry the sexton, angry at having to fill in for Lester.

"Where's Lester?" asked Cecelia Farmer. The rest of the room echoed "Where's Lester, Where's Lester, Where's Lester?"

They were fond of the crusty night sexton, but also missed his strong coffee and the valet service he offered between the church and the parking lot two blocks away. Robert wanted to be honest but could only bring himself to say, "He's taking a little break. Remember, he's been here just about a year and deserves one."

Next the questions turned to the recent murders and the development project he'd talked about in the sermon. The questions came fast and furious.

"Where will the food bank go?"

"What about Nick's Place at the Old Rectory? That's how we help people living on the streets."

"And if we build a condo, they're not going to want street people using the laundry room or playing cards in the lobby. "

"And don't forget the people Dr. Lucy helps to get medical care. "

"And the people Ms. Evans helps on the computer."

"And the kids' playroom."

The session had gone on an hour, and Robert was exhausted. He brought things to a close, saying they'd reconvene next week.

On the way home in their only car, with Molly driving, Robert slumped in his seat and said, "Nobody asked us about our honeymoon. And my birthday's next week. I wonder if anybody will remember."

"I'll remember, dear," answered Molly.

Robert turned to her with a smile. "OK, I'll stop the poor Robert routine. How can I be unhappy married to you?

Chapter Fourteen

~

It was Robert's day off, but he stopped by the church to see what was going on. He lingered a bit and was drinking a cup of tea and rearranging the piles of paper on his office floor when Adele stepped in and closed the door.

"Father, Mr. Stern from the Homeless Coalition is in the reception area. He's come to pick up some papers he left the other day. He's not happy because there's a long line waiting for bus vouchers and I wouldn't let him come to the front. I wondered if you wanted to see him."

"I sure do. Let me find his stuff; it's here somewhere. And we'll have you confuse him by offering VIP escort treatment."

She ushered Gerry in, offered to take his canvas coat and asked if he wanted tea.

He backed away from her, clutching his coat. "No, no, I just want my—"

"Gerry, good to see you again!" Robert reached out his hand. Gerry gave it a swipe.

"Look, just give me the papers, I'm in a hurry."

Robert said, "Here they are," then pulled them back. "Oh, is this the official name of your organization? And your contact information? Wait just a sec while I jot it down, so we can put you on our mailing list."

"I don't want to be—"

"Yes, but I'm sure some of the campers will want to know about our services." Robert chuckled. "Not just the church services; also the vouchers, the sack lunches from the food bank, things like that."

Gerry started to grab the papers back, but Robert had turned and put them on his desk.

"Just a minute; this darn pen isn't working. Hey, I hear the march to protest the Green Streets Initiative has been called off. What are your next steps?"

Gerry said, "It's a good thing the fence is up. We all just want to be left alone."

Robert couldn't help himself. "Oh, have you moved out of your apartment into the jungle?" He didn't expect an answer.

Gerry finally got his hands on the papers and turned to leave. "Don't bother bringing in the waste cans and other stuff. Like I said, they want to be left alone. When the time is right, we'll take our action."

"Sounds exciting," said Robert. "Keep me posted. You and your group are in our prayers." He didn't expect a reply and didn't get one.

When Gerry was gone, Robert asked Adele, "What is it about that guy that makes me want to punch him in the nose?"

"I—I met others like him when I attended the University in the '70s" she said. "Intelligent, pre-occupied with the big issues of the day but unwilling to undertake the hard work involved in addressing those issues, either on the macro or micro level. Oh dear, I've drifted into social work language."

Seeing Robert's nodding encouragement, she continued. "They over-identified with what they called "the people" and the impulsiveness and violence of some of those people. I'm not saying that Mr. Stern has gone that far, but—I wonder."

IT WAS LUCY'S DAY TO STAFF Nick's place, the drop-in center located in the Old Rectory. Uncharacteristically, there were no visitors. It was as if a message had gone out saying today was cleanup day.

Rev. Catherine was there, supervising the decluttering. She knew it was only a matter of time until the fire inspectors came back, and she'd found something for Henry the sexton to do to channel his anger at Lester for taking off. He was methodically removing every single extension cord in the building and already had a garbage can full. She warned Arlis, who secreted the cords she needed to keep her office in operation and herself warm, ahead of time.

Arlis, for her part, was ruthlessly tossing old files; she'd digitized the relevant ones. Then she'd gotten sentimental and digitized a sample of Sunday School Art.

Halfway house residents from across the street were breaking down boxes and delivering items to the trash bins to earn community service hours.

Lucy looked up from her reading as the heavy oak door opened. Spike nosed his way in followed by Lester. Both looked the worse for wear. Spike came over to Lucy and gave her a nuzzle. Lester was holding his jaw.

"Call Chen," he said, "but I want Father Robert or Rev. Catherine here too."

Arlis was at the top of the stairs and ran down when she heard Lester's voice. She detoured to the kitchen and filled a glass and a bowl with water.

Lucy ordered, "Sit down, both of you. Open wide, Lester." He groaned as she gently probed his lower left molars.

"That's a bad abscess. I'll see that you get into the clinic tomorrow and I'll get you a pain killer for now. Arlis, please call Rev. Catherine up from the basement and then contact detective Chen and ask him to come over here."

To Lester, she said, "It's Father Robert's day off but I'm sure he'd come if we called. "

"Nah," he said. "I'd like to spend one more night here before he fires me."

Lucy and Arlis looked at each other and silently decided not to encourage the defeatist in him. Arlis went to the kitchen to search for something for man and dog to eat and to make her calls.

Catherine and Louette raced up the basement stairs, barely missing several broom handles stacked against the wall. Louette ran over to Spike and they exchanged nose rubs.

Catherine placed her face a foot away from Lester's. "Where the hell have you been?" Then she reached over and locked him in a bear hug.

Lucy suppressed a smile, wondering if Lester wished he'd asked for Father Robert instead.

AFTER READING ARLIS' TEXT, RAYMOND CHEN used the opportunity to ride his department-issue scooter up the hill. He was trying it out for the brass to see if it was safe. After three close encounters with vehicles on the steep grade with no bike lane, he reached the top. He pulled onto the grassy patch in front of the Old Rectory.

Arlis was standing in the vestibule when he arrived. He noticed her tears, probably caused by her big heart and too much stimulation, gave a tiny bow and joined the others.

Staring at a point above Lester's head, he said, "Hey man, good to have you back."

Lester reached down, produced a cell phone from somewhere and threw it on the table. It would require coaxing before he'd volunteer anything more, and Raymond was deciding on his approach when Rev. Catherine intervened.

"Where did you get that?" she demanded. `

"Catherine, dear, I think we should leave the questioning to the detective," said Lucy.

"It's OK, Dr. Lucy," Lester said. "I know she's been worried about me. Let's just say I found this in the jungle."

As Raymond decided on his approach, he was armed with information he'd discovered the day before. He'd managed to contact Lester's friend Pete at the Salish Center.

Pete had been sitting in a circle with his apprentices, all carving clan images from their tribes. Raymond was glad that his cultural tradition also valued patience, because it was an hour before the group sheathed their tools.

After they'd exchanged greetings, Raymond said, "I was here yesterday. Nobody would cop to your whereabouts."

"I've been in and out. I saw Les and Spike a few days ago. I heard he'd been doing a walkabout. That's the term the aboriginal Australians use." He waved vaguely toward the jungle.

"I think he was deciding whether to stay or go. I told him he could help more in his current position at the church. I told him he still has the respect of the people here."

Raymond asked, "Can you tell me about the knives you use, and the knives fisherman use and other curved knives that someone might carry around here?"

Over the next fifteen minutes, Pete told him.

"Could you tell me how you've been involved in the recent events?"

Pete was silent.

RAYMOND PICKED UP THE PHONE LESTER had dropped on the table. "Found it or got it handed to you? Any idea whose it is?"

"Why don't you just look at its face value," Lester countered.

Arlis, standing in the corner, smiled. Lester could mangle a phrase like no one else.

Raymond tossed the device between one hand and the other, making no effort to preserve any lingering fingerprints, given its grungy condition.

"If I had to guess, I'd say it belonged to the deceased, Mr. Taylor. We can verify by asking his associates or parents. Problem is, without his password or fingerprint, we don't know what's in there. And unfortunately, he's not around to tell us."

"The hell you say." Lester's shoulders slumped and he grabbed his jaw. "I'd like to know how you got hold of this."

Catherine tugged at Raymond's sleeve; the force of the tug bringing him six inches from her face. She jabbed her index finger towards the kitchen.

"Be right back," Raymond said.

"Lester was in the jungle when Mr. Ramos was killed," she whispered. Are you going to have to treat him as a suspect?"

"No, thank God. I know for a fact he wasn't in the area." Thanks to Pete, he thought. "But don't say anything for now."

When they came back, Lucy said quietly, "Lester needs to go to bed now."

MOLLY WAS GETTING READY TO LEAVE work when a text came in. At the same time, Bishop Anthony called for her over the intercom. She peeked at her phone on the way to his office. The text was from Arlis. Lester was back.

"Bishop?"

"Molly!" they spoke simultaneously.

"You go first," said Molly.

"No, you, dear," said the Bishop. "Beauty before age." He paused. "You know, Marion tells me I need to—"

"Not a bad idea," said Molly. "But I'll take you up on your offer to go first. I just got a text saying our night sexton Lester is back. He's been missing for days. I've got to let Robert know."

"Go ahead. I was just going to tell you the score of the hockey game.

You know, since I announced my retirement, I have more free time. The Diocese seems to be managing itself nicely on its own."

"You're leaving our churches in wonderful shape. And I think it's natural for things to slow down during a transition. I hope you take advantage of the opportunity to focus on the favorite parts of your job," Molly put diplomatically.

He jumped up, almost tripping on the stair that raised his desk a foot off the floor. "That's a stellar idea, Molly. I think I'll schedule a visit to St. Peter's when the Steelhead are running on the Chehalis River. I'll plan a river blessing ceremony with Fr. Marsh and the tribal elders. It's their river you know, and they charge an arm and a leg to fish it."

He noticed that Molly was bouncing back and forth on her feet.

"Oh, sorry, dear—I mean, Molly—you contact Robert and then go on home."

AFTER LEAVING THE CHURCH, ROBERT HAD made a home visit to Deacon Mary and her husband Joe, who was recuperating from a cracked elbow received while pursuing his beer making hobby. The injury allowed Robert to count this as a pastoral visit—a pastoral visit made more sociable by the home brewed amber ale Joe offered.

First, Joe explained how beer making could result in a cracked elbow (involving a quick turn from a worktable into a support column), and then they both decided Joe would live, fortified by a prayer for speedy recovery.

"Now, friend, I need some advice," Robert announced. Joe was a former military officer and seasoned fraud investigator. He'd been a big help during the events of the past two years and the accompanying existential issues that had plagued Robert—guilt that loose stones from their unstable bell tower caused a death and anguish after a friend and parishioner was murdered.

Robert began, "Now that there've been two more murders nearby, the development of our corner property on is on hold. It will be great to have Catherine's help with the mechanics of all that, and I think we can reach a compromise between the competing interest groups,—"

"But?"

Robert turned to his right and left, as if he were looking for an escape route. "But, but, since I've married Molly and had some time away, I feel like chucking it all."

"That's not surprising," said Joe. "You've been through these deaths and the repair, really the reconstruction, of the bell tower. You're a little young for traditional retirement but I know you're not hurting for bucks. For what it's worth, I think you have another one or two projects left in you. But a big redevelopment doesn't need to be one of them, and you don't need to be the rector of Grace Parish to do the good work you want to do."

Mary laughed. "You could be an itinerant preacher, a chaplain to the homeless, a thorn in the side of the powers that be or all three at once! Seriously, I think that Catherine can step up as rector, so long as you're around for guidance. Hmmm, but how would that work? Wait, I've got it! Over the next few years, you could be co-rectors and then you could transition to Rector Emeritus. I'll be 72 next year which is the official retirement age for deacons, but if the Bishop gives his OK, I'll still be a member of congregation and can help too."

Joe re-entered the conversation. "Neither one of you want to live the high life. Maybe a few months a year in the sun. I agree that a mentoring role would suit you. But I have another question, which I had to answer when I was seeing a psychologist." Seeing Robert's round eyes, Joe said, "Oh, yes, when I left the military and started my civilian career, I couldn't hold down a job. Civilians don't like to be ordered around, and I didn't know any other way to communicate. Mary ordered me to see a therapist, who'd been a military officer too. Steve, his name was. After I'd been bellyaching for a few weeks, Steve asked me, 'What's under the rock?'"

Robert gave a little shudder. "You mean, like at the beach when you kick a rock and some weird crustacean scuttles out?"

"I guess you could say that. Anyway, in my case, what was underneath the rock was a very vulnerable crab. I won't bore you with the details. Suffice it to say, once I learned to loosen up, my job retention skyrocketed. I'll bet you've got something underneath your rock too."

"OK, I'll play." Robert sat up straighter. "Let's see, my issue is wanting to chuck it all and run away with Molly but knowing how irresponsible that would be. The word that comes to me is ashamed. Let me think why. Probably because I grew up as an over-indulged, clever little boy with thick glasses. I loved to pretend, and I loved being a know it all. After I finished seminary and was ordained, I got by mostly on, I guess you could call it, my charm. I was able to talk anyone into doing whatever I didn't want to do. And now I seem to have talked Catherine into shouldering this big development project. Leaving me to do what I love, conducting the liturgy and schmoozing. But now I'm ashamed of taking the easy way out. Since the murders, I've tried to do a 180 and turn into Father Responsible, but it's not that easy. All my little guy is able to do is run around in circles."

The phone rang. It was Molly calling to say that Lester had come back. As Mary drove him up the hill to the Old Rectory, she said, "My dad had a great phrase, which can apply to you. The saying was, 'We're off and crawling.' What do you think?"

"I think he had a good sense of humor," answered Robert.

AFTER CHECKING IN WITH LUCY, ROBERT ran up the stairs to Lester's attic bedroom, which used to be his. He stopped at the doorway to get his bearings. Did he really need to save the piles of vintage Mad magazines still on the shelves? Maybe Catherine's acquaintance from the bus would like them.

Spike raised himself from the braided rug and came forward to nuzzle Robert's hand but made it clear by the set of his ears that Lester was not to be awakened.

Robert looked over at the man whom he'd first encountered in a sleeping bag in the church's Memorial Garden. He'd been worried for the past year that Lester wouldn't be able to handle the straight life.

Thank goodness Lucy had told him what bad physical shape Lester was in. He'd been so busy getting him off the streets and putting him to work that he hadn't noticed the bad teeth, poor eyesight, and low weight.

Grace Church needed a wellness program. Other churches had parish nurses, and goodness knows their congregation included enough yoga teachers, masseuses and other health practitioners to staff a spa. A new member had even introduced herself as an aromatherapist. Maybe he could consult with her on incense. Lester wouldn't subject himself to a massage, but others would, and Lester might appreciate a chiropractic adjustment.

Lester snorted so loudly that he woke himself up. Seeing Robert, he reached out his hand. Robert moved forward and grabbed it, without interference from Spike.

"Padre, it sure is good to be back in my own bed—or any bed, for that matter. Do you think I can stay one or maybe two more nights, until I get this tooth pulled? And after that, I'll probably be arrested for killing that guy Ramos."

Robert put on a puzzled face.

"You didn't kill him, did you?" Without waiting for an answer, he asked, "You're thinking of leaving? Have you found a better paying job? You know, it's about time for you to move to step two on our salary scale."

"Ha ha ha." Lester was angry.

"Calm down, buddy. I forgot you don't like sarcasm. Look, I figure you took a few days' vacation to think some things over and maybe do a little investigating on your own."

Lester was wary. He sat up.

"Sure, it would have been nice if you'd told someone," Robert continued, and you'll have to make things up with Henry. The only thing I ask is that you tell Detective Chen everything you know. I'd also like your help recruiting your community contacts for our steering committee on developing this corner property. And don't worry, even when this rectory is gone, we'll need someone living on site."

Lester Jones cracked his knuckles.

"Well, padre, we'll see. Community contacts. I like that."

Chapter Fifteen

~~~

Aғᴛᴇʀ ᴍᴀᴋɪɴɢ sᴜʀᴇ ᴛʜᴀᴛ Rᴏʙᴇʀᴛ ᴡᴏᴜʟᴅ be reunited with Lester, Molly called it a day and drove home through the Washington Park Arboretum, thinking it was the most beautiful commute on earth. The last of the fall leaves on the oaks and maples blazed in the late afternoon light.

Robert had been over the moon to hear that Lester was back. She hoped he wouldn't be devastated if their formerly homeless staff member returned to life on the streets.

She decided to plant some fall flowers in the pots on the deck, since she was sure Robert would be late getting home. He'd already lugged the plants and potting soil up the stairs.

As she opened the slider to the deck, her reverie ended. The green metal chairs had been upended. Red cushions carpeted the floor. The large pots holding her late summer flowers lay in pieces. Stems, leaves and petals stuck up from the soil at crazy angles. Even last night's windstorm couldn't have caused this much damage.

The only thing upright was the round table. The contents of its centerpiece pot spilled all over the surface, but there was something else, a rock with a piece of paper underneath. She thought of running back into the house and locking all the doors. Robert and the police could take it from here.

But she didn't. The rock had been placed at the top of the paper, so she could read the message without touching anything.

To the preacher and his lovely wife. You think your house with its path to the lake is safe because this is a nice part of town. See how easy it is to trespass? If you and your greenie friends don't stop trespassing in our forest, we'll visit again, and this time we'll come inside.

She ran back into the house, slammed the slider shut, shoved the lock into place and punched 911 into her phone.

BILL BAILEY WAS GROGGY. HE'D BEEN monitoring the scanners most of last night. A freak windstorm had swept the Shoreline area, about three miles North of downtown. One person had been killed by a falling tree and power lines were down all over. No one was going anywhere in or out of the area.

He decided on an easy task, tabulating the Halos and Pitchforks received at the Central Seattle website over the past week. Halos represented thanks offered by readers to others in the community. Pitchforks were grumbles about things causing inconvenience to the poster. He was often a recipient of one or the other, along the lines of *Thanks for the great reporting on the tugboat accident,* or *Because you couldn't be bothered to post the detour on 35th, I was late to work.*

This week, he awarded halos to citizens who'd returned lost wallets and phones or paid ahead for a whole line of latte orders. Pitchforks came second. Bill always made sure there were fewer of them. This week's were mostly concerned about the dog poop on the sidewalks.

Next, he reviewed the new queries and comments. The poster making threats against homeless campers was at it again. Bill got the creeps every time he read one. Today, the message referenced the National Guard and bulldozers. He felt in his aching bones that the poster lived nearby-very nearby. The cops hadn't been able to track him. If he could get a handle on the guy's agenda, he'd feel better. The site moderators had given Arlis and him blanket authority to block the comments, but the same sentiments were appearing more frequently from other posters, thankfully without the threats.

No one could deny that things were worse on the streets. Even law-abiding campers were carrying knives for protection, and drug use was sky high. His old crippled body could be out there before too long if his rent went up again.

Finally, Bill checked his email. That was boring, so he checked his junk mail. He was going to sign off soon. His fingers were tingling, his back was seizing up and he needed to get some food in him.

Just before hitting delete, he noticed a subject line including the word cop. There was a video attached.

Whoa! A side view of a man waving around a large knife, maybe even a sword, curved upward at the end. He looked like a crazed warrior in a B-movie. The scenery in the background looked like the jungle, lots of brush and evergreens. The guy was advancing toward someone or something and he got the impression there were others around. The video ended before he could see the victim, if there was one.

He'd seen Chen go into the Old Rectory awhile back, so he texted Arlis, *something big's come in but I can't say what. Can you get the detective over here?*

Before pushing send, he paused. Why not? *and Rev. Catherine?"* He wanted his new acquaintance to see his place, to make sure that she didn't mind being friends with someone living in a dump.

Five minutes later, Raymond and Catherine crossed the street to Bill's apartment building. It was a chilly day, but the front door was open. So were most of the other doors off the hallway. Smells and sounds were bouncing around in a companionable way. Bill called them in from the first door on the left. Catherine made the introductions.

Bill said, "Excuse me not standing up. We'd be wasting five minutes."

"Good one," answered Raymond.

"I have one question before we look at this. Why me? I know I live vicariously through the scanners and posts, but it's a bitch being on the receiving end of all the anti-homeless comments since these two murders. So, do you recognize this guy with the sword?"

Before this moment, Raymond realized, he'd been pretending to be a big city detective, hoping that he'd grow into the role. Like it or not, he now was one, and his next actions needed to be deliberate, not off the hip.

He looked. "Yeah, I know who he is; it's the second victim. We posted his picture, but it didn't get much play. Mr. Ramos was a sometime dock-worker and petty crook with no known family or associates."

He phoned in to headquarters and was able to forward the video for analysis. Then, contradicting the resolution he'd just made, and against department protocol, he began speculating in front of Bill and Rev. Catherine. They were probably at least as smart as his squad mates.

"I wonder who sent this?" he asked.

Bill answered, "Someone who doesn't want to come forward but wants to pin the first murder on Ramos."

"And since he's dead, they hope the police will drop the case," Catherine added."

"It could be they want us to double down and get to the bottom of this," Raymond countered. "They hope we'll find the mastermind of this sleazy operation, which is looking more and more like a criminal enterprise using the jungle to deal drugs. In my wildest imagination I can't imagine the first victim Mr. Taylor being knifed by someone who hated environmentalists."

Bill cracked his neck. "Yea, the jungle's a swell place for drop offs and pickups. I hear it's got lots of old paths, including one which connects to a route under the freeway."

Raymond nodded, and started a search on his phone. "The guys and gals camping over there must know something, and some of them are probably involved. But not all. I'll bet there's some big-time intimidation going on. I'll need to talk to Lester again."

Catherine added, "You may want to locate Murph, the guy who came to the meeting that Father Robert held. There was something strange in the air that day. I guess you could say that Louette and I sniffed it out. Dr. Lucy spent some time with Murph afterwards and she may have picked up something too."

"Thanks a lot for calling us," Raymond said to Bill as he and Catherine left. "Get some sleep, man, but first watch for a pizza delivery coming your way."

Catherine had been interested in the state of Bill's apartment. The one room barely held a twin bed, his computer apparatus, a rolling office chair, a small refrigerator, and a microwave. The bathroom must be down the hall.

The ceilings were high and had their original molding, and the floors were the original fir. It was one of a cluster of historic buildings in the area.

One block up the hill was a big rambling house which had been divided into offices, next door to a two-story brick building built for an early 20th century fraternal group. Its first floor was now the charming coffee house where once a week she abandoned McDonald's and enjoyed a latte with her weekly Coffee with the Rev. discussion group.

The new retirement community towered over them all, and she worried that Grace Church's plan to replace the Old Rectory with multi-story housing would start a chain reaction, even though the housing would be for low to medium income tenants. Grace Church desperately needed the development funds to keep itself upright, but at what cost to the neighborhood's history, and, as their young organist Daniel reminded them, its parish.

ROBERT HAD BEEN UPSTAIRS WITH LESTER when Raymond and Catherine went over to Bill's. When he came back down, accompanied by Spike, he found Dr. Lucy and Louette playing *Guess Which Hand has the Chewy Toy* and Arlis reading a text. The dogs went off the explore the kitchen floor for crumbs.

"Mon Dieu!" said Arlis, forgetting her resolution to stick to her native tongue. During the past week, she'd decided that her love and expression of all things French was more irritating than endearing. She accepted that her student days were behind her, but it would take a while for the transition to be complete.

Robert was walking around the table, part of his resolution to stay active. "What's up?"

She told them about the video Bill had received.

He plopped down on the nearest chair. "It was foolhardy of Mr. Taylor to wander into that area, but how could he know that he'd run into a guy with a knife? The only good thing, I guess, is the police have something more to work with."

Arlis' cell burst into song. Of course, she'd chosen "Le Marseillaise."

"It's Molly. Please, I need to find Robert. He's not answering his cell."

Before doing anything, Arlis snuck a look at her rector. Molly seemed beyond upset; she was choking on her words. Arlis tried to speak calmly.

"Don't worry, he's right here."

She handed the phone to Robert and signaled to Dr. Lucy that something was wrong.

"Aghhh! Molly! Call the police! I'll be right there. Lock all the doors! Oh God, help us!" He slammed the phone on the table, jumped up and started to run out the front door of the Old Rectory.

"Father Robert! Stop!" Lucy commanded.

Arlis picked up the phone and asked Molly what had happened.

"I, I got home from work and, and someone had been on our deck. They turned over the pots and furniture and left a, a, scary message, like a threat against both of us. What the He-ck is going on at the church? I, I never thought—No! Don't say that to Robert! Just, I need him here!"

"Yes, yes," soothed Arlis. "Right away. I'll stay on the phone with you.

I just need to give Dr. Lucy my car keys."

Her vintage Citroen was right out front, thank God. And thank God that Raymond, escorting Rev. Catherine, was coming through the front door. His scooter wouldn't help him now.

RAYMOND DROVE THE CITROEN, ENJOYING THE vintage shifting mechanism, while Dr. Lucy tried to keep Robert calm in the tiny back seat.

"Robert, I know how upset you are, but when we get there you need to be strong for Molly."

"How can I?" he wailed. "I've put her in danger by meddling with things that aren't my business."

Although she'd heard the story many times, Dr. Lucy listened again as he recounted how he'd had to wait until his 50's to find the love of his life. His two other serious relationships had been with women who'd chosen their career over marriage to a somewhat itinerant preacher. His first wife was a physician who refused to leave her residency, and his second relationship was with a parishioner at his Portland, Oregon church who decided to devote her life to environmental work.

Lucy knew that Molly could have succeeded in any number of careers but had chosen the stability of a partnership with her late husband. Because he made a comfortable living as a physician, Molly had been able to volunteer for the causes they both believed in. Lucy also knew that when Molly and Robert met, she was the Bishop's unpaid secretary, and had shepherded Robert through the challenges of being a new rector in the Seattle diocese.

Robert had told her that Molly's auburn hair, curvy figure and mischievous smile entranced him. She'd found a shade of red that complemented her hair and complexion and rarely wore any other color. Her wardrobe ranged from jeans to mid-level couture, and she enjoyed advising the women she mentored on developing their personal style. He'd tried not to treat her as a precious doll, as the Bishop and many others did, but hadn't been entirely successful. Molly had supported him through two deaths at Grace Church, one a vicious murder, and an attempt on his life. It seemed like a miracle that someone of her distinction would want to marry him.

When they pulled into the driveway, Robert extricated his hand from Lucy's and raced up the front steps.

Molly was sitting in the big leather chair her late husband had loved.

She was wearing a fluffy red bathrobe, which she ordinarily wouldn't dream of putting on before bedtime. She greeted him with, "I've never been afraid here before."

Robert knelt on the floor in front of her, crying, just as he'd done last year when he saw his friend Nick dead in the Old Rectory.

It didn't take Raymond and the police responder long to figure out how the person got on the deck. A ladder had been conveniently stored underneath. They could see the holes it had made in the rain drenched ground when it was raised up. Anyone passing by would think someone was doing a repair.

Raymond and the officer collected evidence and then left with Lucy. Molly and Robert would follow after they packed. They were going to stay temporarily in a vacant condo in Deacon Mary and Joe's building.

BACK AT HER STUDIO APARTMENT LOCATED at the Heritage House Retirement Community, Dr. Lucy greeted her kitties, Stella and Luna and then put on her most comfortable slippers. Even with Raymond's help, it had been hard getting down the steps at Molly and Robert's home. It was almost time to go to the dining room if she wanted dinner. Tonight, the theme was Italian, one of her favorites. But maybe she'd just heat up a can of soup on her tiny stove.

Why, after such an event filled day, was she feeling a letdown? There, she'd answered her own question. She was satisfied that she'd been able to help, as she had so many times in her adult life. She had a close relationship with her brother and niece, and had many, almost too many, friends from her church and volunteer work. But at the end of the day, it was just her and the kitties.

THE DESIGNATED GREEN STREET A BLOCK above Grace Church looked as though a hurricane had come through. Young trees, shrubs and plants that had been nestling in meandering rain gardens had been uprooted and were strewn all over. So had the supplemental drip irrigation tubes.

The eco-friendly benches had been torn off their foundations. Waste receptacles were overturned. Whoever was responsible posted a sign at Green Street Alliance headquarters saying *Stay out of the jungle or the rest of your green streets will be next.* They posted the same message on the Central Seattle message board.

When Robert heard about the desecration the next morning, he ran up to look. Sure enough, there wasn't any space to walk, given the mess on the sidewalks.

Robert ran back to his office and relayed what Gerry Stern had told him about 'taking action' to the police, but it turned out that Mr. Stern had an alibi. He'd been at a medical clinic the evening before getting treatment for a dislocated shoulder. It must have been some other group.

The other homeless groups contacted by police said they welcomed the street amenities and wouldn't think of doing such a thing. And there things stood.

Chapter Sixteen

~~~

Raymond Chen set the alarm earlier than usual, showered, slicked down his hair, put on the shirt and pants his grandmother had carefully laundered in return for his shopping services, and had an extra cup of coffee. He was the first in the room at headquarters for the case conference on the Jungle Murders.

Lieutenant Olson wasted no time. "These needed to be solved yesterday. The mayor is announcing a new homeless initiative, but not until this mess is out of sight and out of mind. What have you got, Detective Collins?"

Ben Collins, the case lead, said, "I'm letting Detective Chen report. He's done all the work." The Lieutenant's raised brows indicated that Ben had some explaining to do later.

Raymond kept a straight face and gave a concise summary of the investigation to date, giving credit to the team for the little work they'd done on his advice. He also credited the help provided by "neighborhood groups," especially the video of Mr. Ramos.

He hoped he wouldn't have to get more specific about his sources at this point. The lieutenant might be skeptical of evidence provided by a scanner jockey, a church bookkeeper, and a homeless camper. And then there was Lester, who'd irritated Lieutenant Olson to no end during the investigations of the previous deaths at the church. This next part would be tricky. "Maybe this is off base, but I think the key here is corralling the bad guys who've been operating a drug operation in the jungle—and I don't mean the campers."

Hearing no objection, he continued, "According to the campers willing to talk, someone's running the operation near the place where Mr. Taylor's body was found. They probably figure a forest is a better hideout than a drug house up on Beacon Hill. From what I've been able to gather, the dealers are supplying just enough product to the addicts who live in the jungle to buy their silence and have intimidated most of the rest. But I, we've, managed to find one, maybe two guys willing to help."

He paused for reaction. There was none, so he continued, "But before we're ready to go, there's the question of where the stuff is coming from and who the ringleaders are. And what role Ramos was playing, and of course, who killed him."

"Any ideas?" asked the lieutenant, specifically to the rest of the team.

"That's not much to go on," ventured the female team member, Marilee Moore.

"That answer's not good enough," answered the Lieutenant.

Raymond continued, "I'd hate to think the stuff's coming from the fishing fleet, because that hasn't been a problem before now. Ramos had done some fishing, but it's more likely the stuff was arriving via trucks or tankers. It's obvious Ramos was involved, but who else?"

"What about those native carvers?" asked Lieutenant Olson, and to Raymond's dismay, continued, "Their tribal center is on the South side of the jungle, and we all know how they like to wave their knives around." He was referring to the police shooting of one such carver a few years previously, the incident that Raymond and Lester had discussed at the beginning of the case.

"Actually, lieutenant," interjected Ben Collins, "the video backs up the pathologist. Dr. Ahn said the murder weapon was larger than a woodcarving knife and most filleting knives. As a matter of fact, it looks like some kind of ceremonial weapon. It really fries me that some unsuspecting out of town nerd had to be on the receiving end."

The lieutenant slapped his hand on the table. "Now that you all finally seem to be arriving on the same page, get out there and work your contacts on the waterfront, the port, the jungle and at that blas- blessed church. No time off, no off-duty gigs, no kids' soccer games until you get results."

The rest of the team were gone by the time Raymond and Ben got to the hallway.

"I doubt our teammates think we're on the same page," Raymond commented.

"Yea, well, this is Friday and they probably had plans for the weekend. I know that Ornette was going to work the Seahawks game on Sunday. They'll be waiting in the cafeteria."

Raymond and Ornette usually got along because they shared the same taste in music. Ornette's dad had been one of the best sax players to come out of Seattle and had named his son after one of the greats.

When he and Ben sat down with the others, Raymond took a chance. "Hey Jazz Man, I'll bet you $50.00 that you make the Seahawk's game."

"Oooh, that's cool, bro." Ornette tipped an imaginary hat. "And even if I miss the game, I sure could use that 50."

Raymond didn't know where he got the courage to say, "Take it or leave it, man. I have the name of a guy who's supposed to be dealing these folks' stuff at the upper part of the forest in your territory. I'm sure you know him."

Ornette pretended to be outraged. "That Twit? He owes me one too many. After he talks and signs on the dotted line, I'm putting him on a bus back home."

Raymond had other names and addresses for the team members who worked the waterfront and points south.

Ben Collins slapped his hand softly on the cafeteria table.

"Let's go."

Rev. Catherine and Father Robert met Friday morning at his temporary digs in the downtown high-rise condo. Molly had insisted on going to work despite yesterday's frightening experience and Deacon Mary was holding down the fort at the church.

"I don't think I've ever been this high up in my life, except for airplanes," Catherine said, looking out the oversized windows on the 24th floor.

Robert was set to launch into a business discussion about the church's future but paused when he saw the look on her face.

"What do you see, Catherine?"

"I see, I see—everything's shimmering. It doesn't matter that I can't make out every detail, although I think that's one of the ferries. Why can't everyone enjoy a view like this?"

Robert joined her. A shaft of sun spotlighted the ferry on its way to Bainbridge Island.

He said, "Let's invite some of the others over this evening, also Raymond and his team. We can enjoy the view and try to get to the bottom of these murders."

"And let's also invite Bill and Murph, " she added.

STARTING AT FIVE P.M., A GROUP of people entered the lobby of the downtown condo where Fr. Robert and Molly were staying temporarily. Some had taken the bus, one had walked, others came by taxi or one of the alternatives.

Deacon Mary and her husband Joe, who lived in the same condo, welcomed the guests, and made sure everyone found the elevator.

The guests were greeted at the door of unit 2417 by Molly. She took their coats, umbrellas and backpacks and ushered them into the great room with its splendid view of the Space Needle, Puget Sound, and the Harbor. Dr. Lucy offered appetizers and drinks from a well-stocked counter. Daniel played softly on the grand piano.

After a half hour of enjoyment, Robert invited everyone to take a seat. The three couches, five easy chairs and eight dining chairs provided more than enough. The guests included Seattle detectives Raymond Chen, Ben Collins and Merrily Moore; also, Bill, Lester, Murph and Pete the carver.

Robert welcomed them. "Ordinarily I'd start with a prayer but there's no need. The view, the light, the delicious food, the music, the artwork and all of you are prayer enough.

"On to the case at hand. We need to find out who murdered Mr. Taylor and Mr. Ramos. But that's not enough. We need to get rid of the forces—that's all I can think to call them—that have been infecting our community, or, as Daniel has reminded us, our parish. As I've said before, Grace Church is located at a crossroads, between old and new, rich and poor, and people of all sorts of backgrounds. It should be a place of hope, of reconciliation, of—"

"Tell it, Father!" yelled Lester.

Robert took that as his signal to shut up and turned things over to Detective Chen.

"Sorry for having to talk murder in the middle of all this beauty," said Raymond, "but let's start by comparing notes.

"Murph here was an eyewitness to Ramos committing the first murder. Murph, don't worry, you don't need to say anything more. Thank you, Dr. Lucy, for encouraging Murph to come forward. We also have a video sent anonymously to the Central Seattle website."

Raymond's fellow detectives looked down at their hands.

Raymond continued, "We've learned from the Filipino Center that Mr. Ramos had exhibited signs of mental illness. He developed a fixation on the traditions of his ancestors and had started carrying a ceremonial weapon. The ringleader of the operation had recruited him to distribute drugs out of the jungle to dealers around the area. Ramos must have snapped when he saw the alien Mr. Taylor with his hiking attire and latte. Taylor was probably also taking pictures with his phone, which Lester managed to recover.

"As to who killed Ramos, we think we know but still have to prove it. The suspect has an alibi for the time. He could have had someone else do it but from what we know about him, thanks to Paul and Merrily, he wanted the thrill and needed to silence the crazy Mr. Ramos. We have to break the alibi. Our next step is to pressure his associates."

"I offer myself to help with that," said Lester. "Thanks to the caring I've received at the church, I'm fully recovered from my recent bout of PTSD."

"Let's keep it that way," answered Raymond. "Besides, I understand from Rev. Catherine that your help is needed to get ready for the upcoming fire inspection at the Old Rectory."

Bill, who didn't know Lester well, made the mistake of snorting.

Lester had been sprawled on the eight-foot-long leather couch. He sat up and got the look in his eye that had intimidated many an associate in the past. His dog Spike wasn't around to calm him down.

Raymond improvised quickly. "But more important, you can work with Murph to ID the campers who aren't involved in the drug operation. We don't care if they took advantage of some free product."

After thirty seconds, Lester said, "I can do that."

Robert said, "Raymond, it sounds like your team has what's needed to make an arrest. Let's adjourn, finish up the appetizers and catch the last of the sunset."

RAYMOND LINGERED AFTER THE OTHERS LEFT. "Father, can we talk some more about the murders?"

"Yes, and I'm glad you're asking, because I've had a real struggle with my role in all this, with these murders and the others too. I'm the rector of Grace Church, supposedly in charge, but everything's been swirling around, totally out of my control. And I think maybe you and Joyce felt the same way." Detective Joyce Hitchcock had been assigned to the first two deaths and was now part of the chief's staff.

Robert continued, "I think you'll agree that my little team here at Grace has tended to go off on their own, forgetting to check in with headquarters."

Raymond was checking a text. "Father, believe me, I'm listening, but I'm on duty and have to stay tuned in. And yes, it has been chaotic." He put down his phone and smiled. "Remember how Mae dressed like a bag lady to infiltrate the food bank line? And how Lester and Pete climbed to the top of the bell tower so they wouldn't feel inferior to everyone else and then ended up being suspects in Clare's death?"

Robert added, "And how Daniel used his eidetic vision to identify the person who threw the stone off the bell tower and then later identified Nick's killer by the sound of his car keys? I notice this time Daniel's sticking to playing calming music on the piano."

Robert had eased himself onto the leather couch. "Anyway, I've tried this time get everyone to funnel their ideas through me so I could get them to you in one piece. Of course, that didn't work with Lester."

Raymond silenced his phone. "Lester's one of a kind. Otherwise, it's worked. He sat still for a minute, and then told Robert, "Here's who we're arresting. I can give you the probable cause and all that, but for now, tell me what you think."

Robert crossed himself. "I probably have too much compassion for lost souls, but I believe you're right."

Chapter Seventeen

～～

O N A GREY, DRIZZLY SUNDAY MORNING at 7 a.m., Raymond, Ben, Marilee and three patrol backups arrived at a two-story apartment building which rambled over most of its lot. It seemed to have been expanded at least three times. A few semis rumbled by on Commercial Way.

It took them awhile to find right apartment, since many of the upstairs units had individual staircases. After yelling, "Police," and waiting five full seconds, they busted open the door to 7b. They'd had enough probable cause to get a warrant. The suspect came out of a back bedroom. He'd probably slept in the t-shirt and jeans he had on. His arm was in a sling.

They all had their guns out. Shouts of "Freeze!" and "Hands up!" ricocheted around the room.

Before he knew it, Gerry Stern, the head of the criminal enterprise disguised as the Homeless Coalition, was under arrest. Ben frisked him and found a revolver in his pocket. It was the same type that had been used to kill Mr. Ramos.

As Mr. Stern was being led away, Ben growled, "We should have given him a second to go for the gun."

Raymond answered, "Don't you want to hear his story?"

"WHAT'S GERRY STERN'S STORY?" ROBERT ASKED Raymond a week later. I've read the news reports but can't figure out why he chose this kind of life."

"The press has been working overtime on this one," Raymond

answered, "but they're focusing on the sensational stuff, the violence, drugs and homeless issues. Sorry I'm underwater on the job, but I can point you in the right direction if you want to get some background."

Robert, with Adele's help, found that Gerry Stern had grown up as a bright but bored child whose parents provided good schools and a comfortable lifestyle, but perhaps not enough mentoring. He was a voracious reader and as a teen happened upon accounts of the student protests of the late 1960s and early '70s.

The groups which embraced violent action to meet their goals especially appealed to him, groups such as the Weather Underground and the Symbionese Liberation Army. Learning that they often affiliated with ex-cons heightened the excitement factor. After one year of university, Gerry dropped out and learned welding at a community college, the better to ally himself with the real workers.

Along the way, he found common cause with others who'd taken the same path. He had no problem dealing in drugs to fund his cause, which was to enlist their homeless comrades to terrorize the city as a revolutionary action. The invasion of Molly and Robert's deck and destruction on the green street was their first effort.

Gerry was technically correct in saying he wasn't involved in the second action. It turned out that he'd dislocated his shoulder by falling off the ladder he'd used to get onto Robert and Molly's deck. However, he'd directed the operation using communications equipment purchased with proceeds from drug sales.

ROBERT WAS ENJOYING A CUP OF tea with Adele after the morning's research. "Adele, let me see if I remember something from Sociology 101. Don't you think that if Mr. Stern had stayed in university, , he'd have learned that if you're poor, basic survival trumps ideology? The homeless people he wanted to enlist probably put up with him as long as the drugs and a few extra bucks were coming in. He didn't realize that people with Mr. Ramos' background were not inclined to share the spoils."

"Yes," she answered, "and in his paranoid state, Mr. Ramos killed Mr. Taylor in a brutal way. And then he was murdered by Mr. Stern."

Robert's fingers tingled. "And then Gerry, maybe with his friends, or maybe not, hung Mr. Ramos on a chain link fence, just like they did with Matthew Shepherd in Wyoming in the '90s and all the other lynching victims going back in time. Just like Christ on the cross. Guilty or not, no human should endure that indignity."

Later, at home with Molly, Robert couldn't stop talking about what led to Gerry Stern's arrest.

"The campers living above the freeway weren't getting their payoffs or else were tired of the drug dealing and violence. They'd had enough, and as he would put it, ratted him out. But why did he murder Mr. Ramos?"

Molly thought, and then answered, "I think he'd developed a thirst for violence through his contacts over the years. It could also have been a misguided attempt to keep the jungle off-limits to anyone except his revolutionary comrades."

Robert added, "His fantasy was probably to die in a shootout with the pigs, but he had to settle for being handcuffed and booked into jail. You know, if this were a movie, Adele would deserve full credit for the research she's done."

"So, what's happening now?" asked Molly. "I know he's in jail waiting for trial, but does he have an attorney? And what about his parents?"

"Raymond told me that Gerry turned off his cellmates with his rhetoric and got transferred to protective custody. He's in a private cell 23 hours a day and gets let out for an hour in what's called an outdoor exercise area. There's a wall going up about sixteen feet and then a chain link opening letting in some fresh air. And a basketball hoop with no net. He's refused an attorney. He wants to defend himself."

Molly went over to the slider and opened it. Looking out on the reassembled deck, its pots blooming with asters, she said, "I imagine him bouncing a basketball with his good arm while he plans his defense. I know you've applied to visit him and I'm sorry he's refused."

Robert joined her. "I managed to contact his parents today. They're horrified at what their son has become and told me they're both in therapy. I asked if they were coming to Seattle to visit him. They told me they weren't ready."

Chapter Eighteen

~~~

ONE MONTH AFTER MR. STERN'S ARREST for the murder of Mr. Ramos, Father Robert re-convened his task force to plan development of the church's corner property. Rev. Catherine handed out the agenda she'd prepared. Then Robert explained that any decision would need to consider the health of the surrounding community, including the forest, the hospitals, retirement communities and the halfway house.

"Instead of a spoken prayer," he said, "let's be quiet for five minutes, eyes opened or closed."

"Five minutes! No way can I do that!" insisted their development consultant, Ed Grafton.

"Sure, you can, Ed," answered Robert.

Five minutes later, Robert struck a brass bowl with a wooden mallet. The sound reverberated for thirty seconds. He paused for another thirty seconds, and then said, "As we consider our future, we also need to consider our present. We need to realize that homelessness, drug use and crime have gotten worse in the past few years and won't be going away anytime soon. Jesus said the poor will always be with us, but I don't think he meant like this. Terry tells me that people are pulling knives on each other at our food bank, and believe me, it's not over a bag of rice. Deacon Mary reports that people living in the retirement community across the street have been confronted and pushed around while they're out walking their dogs. And we all know when someone over seventy falls, it can be disastrous.

"Where were these desperate people before? Were they in prison, a mental institution, fleabag hotels, riding the rails? Did both the haves and have nots used to be more tolerant of each other? And what about the story of the Good Samaritan? How does it apply here and now?"

A few of the task force members were raring to go and began to speak. Robert raised his hand and said, "Please let me finish. Now we're being called to serve what people think of as the unworthy poor, the ones who live in the middle of trash, carry knives for protection and use them against each other. It's not enough to ring the city with tent camps or build more jails for the unworthy poor. We have to ask, what's our mission moving forward? And before Lester shouts, 'Tell it, Father,' again, I'll turn it over to Ed."

"The first thing I want to do is apologize, again." said Ed.

"I hired a so-called real estate consultant who's just been arrested for sending threatening messages to the Central Seattle message board and a bunch of other things. He's the guy I brought to the last meeting, Mr. Fowler. It turns out he was hoping to buy up property around here from frightened owners and hold it until things calmed down. And to make things worse, the police here tell me he was paying off Mr. Stern, the so-called homeless advocate, to stir things up. He stirred them up alright!

"Of course, you know that last year I was conned by Nick's killer into another development scheme for this property. You'll just have to believe me when I say that I thought I had the church's and food bank's best interests at heart, and I did this time too. From now on I'll try to stick to food distribution."

Stacy Chase, their senior warden, was back from maternity leave and ready to roll. "Get over it, Ed. You're on board now. If, or I guess, when, we tear down the Old Rectory and food bank, there has to be someplace for people to wash their clothes and take a shower and hang out, like they do now at Nick's Place. And these people probably won't be the undeserving poor, although I plan to use that phrase in our marketing literature. They're folks like Bill here, who have a room, but no place to do his laundry and socialize."

Stacy stood up, showing off her restored youthful figure, "I'm going off topic, but let me pass around this picture of baby Charlotte. She said her first word last week, and it wasn't Mama or Da. It was 'Go!' I'm so proud of her!"

"Like mother, like daughter," Robert smiled. "You're next, Lester."

Lester removed his baseball cap. "Thank you for this opportunity to express myself," he said. In spite of my bad behavior in recent days, Father Robert has offered me a second chance, which will require that this new building will need a little bedroom and a bathroom nearby for the night sexton. And his dog."

Raymond noticed that Lester was squinting. He texted Arlis, "The church offers some type of eye insurance, right? Could you get him set up?"

"*Oui*. I mean, yes. You're the fourth person who's asked."

"Thanks. Are you up for dinner later?" he texted back.

"Yes."

Pete from the Salish Center hadn't been at the church for two years, when he and Lester were on the streets. He was mystified that these people considered the forest a part of their parish but wasn't going to refuse when Father Robert asked him to work with the others on a plan for the area. He'd participated in a subcommittee representing tribal, environmental and homeless interests that had met earlier. They knew it would be difficult to negotiate with the state transportation officials who controlled the forest area but had developed a list of enhancements, including spaces for a sweat lodge and drumming circle, a forest management program, and a few paths.

"Our people probably never slept in the forest. Too steep. Maybe some hunting. It wasn't used for burial sites. Those were on the edge of what's now called Lake Washington." His braid swung over his shoulder as he turned towards Raymond. "Detective Chen knows, and Lester knows, that a few of us moved Mr. Taylor's body to a more suitable place, surrounded by cedar trees."

"And then set the fire so his body would be found," said Robert. Since it hadn't been a question, Pete didn't answer.

Ed Grafton jumped in again. "That's something else that really fries me. Mr. Ramos and his friends left a bunch of trash and drug paraphernalia at the place where Mr. Taylor was murdered. They wanted everyone to pin the murder on the homeless bums. And then Stern turned against his so-called homeless friends and took money from my so-called associate to do just that."

It was Murph's turn. Murph looked at Lucy.

She translated, "People, like Murph, who are living in the forest, or parks, want solitude and love being outdoors, except in bad weather. They hate having things disrupted. How hard would it be to accommodate their lifestyle? And by the way, I have a friend in Canada who did figure out a way. He ran a residential facility in the countryside and let anyone who wanted to sleep outdoors. I'll give the details to the subcommittee."

"Thank you so much, Dr. Lucy, Robert said. The ones we call the unworthy poor need care also. I'm thinking of the original hospitals and monasteries who took in the ones with nowhere to go and probably didn't use drug tests as a barrier to entry."

He continued, "You could also call them refuges or treatment centers or whatever. In today's world it would have to involve safe, loving care geared to addiction, poor health and childhood trauma."

"I second that," said Rev. Catherine. "But it will involve a larger community than our parish, and Father Robert, I think that's where your heart is. Am I right?"

Robert nodded.

After a pause, Catherine summarized, "I propose that we consider a mid-rise development called Parish House. The lower floors will include common spaces for hanging out and meetings, and there'll also be a deck on top. If the millennials can do it in their condos, so can we. The living units will be accessible for people like me and Bill. And most of them will be affordable on social security and disability."

"Ah, shoot," said Bill. "I was hoping for a name like Gimp Plaza."

"Are you ready for me to go on?" she asked.

"Sorry," said Bill.

"You can probably tell I've been thinking a lot about this. There will also be units for people who can afford more, because why isolate people in enclaves?

"Everyone will contribute to Parish House and the parish in any way they can. For instance, a retired lawyer with a nice pension will help with legal issues. Or a business student with two kids will help Arlis with the bookkeeping. A social service worker will locate affordable childcare and other services. I could go on. But if you'll put your trust in me, knowing that this is exactly where Louette and I would like to live, I promise to work with all of you to make it happen."

She sat back in her chair and turned it over to Mr. Larsen of the Green Streets Alliance.

"That sounds fantastic, Rev. Catherine. All our group asks is that the entrance to the project is set back at the corner and that the sidewalks are wide enough for four people, and that they're bordered by rain garden planting strips. So that would mean no street parking."

Ed Grafton knew that Arlis was next but also knew that she wouldn't object.

"I'm going to speak out of turn and it's not about food. We can't have the folks who live in this building stepping over people passed out on your new wide sidewalk or on the benches I'm sure you also want. With flower-pots in between for everyone to trip over and use for their cigarette butts. And unless you want the residents to be prisoners in their accessible apart-ments, there has to be parking, at least for ride services and Access Vans."

Mr. Larsen countered, "There won't be a need for parking. People will walk, bike or take transit."

Ed countered back, "No they won't. Not everyone. And do you want your charming, narrow streets crowded with cars from the ride services? And scooters terrorizing everyone on your wide sidewalks?"

Mr. Larsen re-countered, "Any parking would need to be under the building and only be accessed from the freeway side." He saw several others ready to jump in and decided to follow the program. "You and I can talk some more later, Ed. Ms. Bell, I think you're up next."

Arlis was texting. "I pass."

Terry from the food bank laughed. He and Arlis had a long history. "Come on, Arlis. Don't you want a nice big office labeled Parish House Administrator?"

"No! Just, uh, maybe a decent heating system."

It was Dr. Lucy's turn, who said, "For once, I have nothing to add, except to relay that Daniel hopes that the common space has room for a piano. And wait! Of course, the building will include a dispensary."

"Do you mean a pharmacy?" asked Molly, who had been pleased to be included.

"Not quite," Lucy answered. "It's a way of getting basic medical ser-vices to people who don't need a hospital but can't wait for a doctor visit. If we want our building to serve all its residents, there needs to be a place they can go for first aid, blood pressure readings, and most important, some TLC."

Bill Bailey, the scanner guy, was next. "Since we're dreaming, if this project included a little communications studio, I could take on a few apprentices."

"OK, I'll be Mr. 'Yes, but' here," said Ed Grafton. "With all the add-ons you're proposing, I figure we now have space for one or two rent-generating apartments."

Robert said to Bill, "There's empty space in the undercroft of the church."

Bill answered, "I don't know what undercroft means, but it sounds like an out of the way place. If I can get in and out on my scooter, and get decent reception, it could work."

Robert turned to Terry, "and you're sure the food bank will have a place?"

"Thanks to Ed, we'll be using part of his warehouse space South of here. It'll work great." Terry looked off into space. "I sure miss Nick. Father, remember the time you came in the upper door to the old gym's running track just when Nick threw the basketball at me? Only he hit you instead and broke your glasses?"

"How could I ever forget," said Robert, touching his tortoise shell rims.

After an appropriate silence, Raymond said, "I know I'm just an observer, but just saying, research shows that if people feel part of a community, things are safer."

"I think that's enough for today," Robert said.

ED GRAFTON AND TERRY HUSTLED OUT first. Places to be, things to do.

Catherine, her service dog Louette, and Bill Bailey headed towards the front door.

"Hey, it's snowing!" said Bill. "It's a good thing my scooter has all weather wheels."

Raymond, Arlis, and Murph and his backpack set out for her car. They were dropping him off at the City Hall cold weather shelter. He'd declined their offer of dinner.

Lester, Pete, and Spike were headed to the dog run over the freeway. "Don't worry, padre," Lester said, "I'll lock up before we go."

Lucy wrapped a scarf around her neck and put on a wool hat, telling Robert and Molly, "I'm looking forward to walking home in the snow. Tonight's my book club."

Robert and Molly walked towards Red's parking space. They hadn't yet decided whether to get a second car.

"Would you drive, dear?" Molly asked. "I know it's a short drive home, but I'm afraid my night vision is going."

He laughed. "So far, I'm OK on that front, but I hope the rest of my vision doesn't get worse. Something to think about for the future. I sure appreciate the Access card Catherine gave me for my birthday."

He slipped on the slushy sidewalk but righted himself quickly with a little hop.

"See, Moll, those balance classes at the Y are doing me some good." He turned around in a circle, surveying the church, the Old Rectory and gym, the half-way house, the retirement tower, and the forest. "But it doesn't hurt that we're standing on solid ground."

"No dear," said Molly, "We're standing on sacred ground."

Photograph by Paul Hannah

KATHIE DEVINY TURNED TO WRITING AFTER a career as social worker and criminal justice manager. As the wife of an Episcopal priest who served a downtown Seattle Parish, she is familiar with the issues raised in her mysteries. Her essays have appeared in *Cure Today* magazine, Bernie Siegel's *Faith Hope and Healing* and *Episcopal Voice*. Kathie and her husband Paul divide their time between the northwest and California.

Now read the first book in the
Grace Church Mystery series

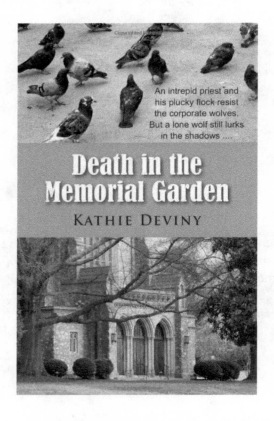

An intrepid priest and
his plucky flock resist
the corporate wolves.
But a lone wolf still lurks
in the shadows ....

**Death in the
Memorial Garden**

KATHIE DEVINY

A box of unidentified ashes is unearthed during an inter-
ment ceremony. With their congregation dwindling and their
world literally falling in around them, Father Robert Vickers
and his colorful staff members and volunteers put their heads
together to solve the mystery of the ashes and find the means
to save Grace Church from the developers ... all in time for
the Bishop's visit.

CPSIA information can be obtained
at www.ICGtesting.com
Printed in the USA
LVHW051840231120
672481LV00009B/2315